Love, Debra

LOVE, DEBRA

a novel by Fritz Hamilton

OPEN HAND PUBLISHING INC.
Seattle, Washington

Open Hand Publishing Inc.
P.O. Box 22048
Seattle, WA 98122
(206) 323-3868

Distributed by
The Talman Company, Inc.
150 Fifth Avenue
New York, N.Y. 10011
(212) 620-3182

Library of Congress Cataloging-in-Publication Data

Hamilton, Fritz.
    Love, Debra.
    Summary: Running away from her sexually abusive father, fifteen-year-old Debra discovers a world of alcohol, drugs, and prostitution which she describes in a series of letters to her dead mother.
    [1. Runaways—Fiction. 2. Prostitution—Fiction. 3. Letters—Fiction] I. Title.
PS3558.A4424L6 1990 813'.54 [Fic] 90-7412
ISBN 0-940880-29-6

ISBN: 0-940880-29-6 paperback
ISBN: 0-940880-30-X cloth cover

Printed in the United States of America
95 94 93 92 91 90 7 6 5 4 3 2 1

For Phoebe, who gave me the love and support without which this book would not have been wrtitten.

Acknowledgment

Special thanks to my editor, Phyllis Hatfield, and to my publisher, Anna Johnson, for the long hours of hard work, and the love and care they both put into the production and birth of this book.

Dear Mom,

I was looking at my calendar and saw that it's the anniversary of your death, when Daddy and I drove you to detox and you died of DTs. So I thought I'd write you this letter to tell you I still love you and miss you, and things are just as horrible here as they always were.

I'll start with the good stuff. I went to the Dairy Queen yesterday, the same one you and I always went to before the drinking got so bad you didn't care anymore. And you know how much I like the chocolate sundaes. Well, this time I got a strawberry shake because that was always your favorite, and I drank it for you.

I think I'll write you more and more now, Mom, because I don't have anybody to talk to here and I have to let somebody know what's going on or I'll go crazy. The kids in this town always have called me crazy, and both Dad and Margo, the waitress he's been living with this year, agree.

Maybe that's because I talk sort of like a grownup and I've always had big breasts, ever since I was 10, and I look as old as their mothers even if I am short. I don't know. All I know is I have no friends here, and they laugh at me, even though I always have the best clothes because Daddy wants everybody to know how rich he is as the president of the lumber company.

1

I know you hate me for mentioning this again, because you beat me up when I first told you and told me never to say it again, but Daddy still makes me take off my clothes in front of him, even if Margo is around. (She likes it too.) He puts me on exhibit like a cow. It really excites him. Then he takes me to bed, usually with Margo there too. And he plays with us both in bed. Margo seems to like it, but I still hate it. I try not to let it make me too sick. I won't talk about this again, because I know how angry it makes you.

Also, I don't know where to send your letter, because I know there's no delivery to Heaven. I also know you couldn't possibly be in the other place where the letter would burn up before you could read it (ha ha).

Anyway, Mom, I'm 15 years old now, and I can't stand it here, being the richest and unhappiest and loneliest girl in this town or maybe in the world. I still read a lot of books, and I don't believe that all those kids could be so happy, like on television. In our family you were always drinking and Daddy always had his women and you were always yelling at each other and beating each other up. And except when you were yelling at me or beating me up, nobody much cared about me, it seemed.

Except the times when you and I would be alone. You don't know how happy it made me after Daddy would go to work, to make you the pancakes and take them in to you when you were just waking up. I would always wait until about noon because you liked to sleep late, and then I'd take them in singing happy birthday to you or something like that.

Maybe you wonder why I've never visited you at your grave. It's because I don't know where you're lying. Daddy would never tell me where they took you. He said you wanted it that way, but I don't believe him. He's just not telling me because he thinks I'm bad, and I guess I am.

Anyway, what I really wanted to ask you is whether it's okay with you if I run away now. I think I can get a job as a waitress someplace, like Margo. Not that I want to do any-

2

thing that she does, because I hate her so much, but I think it's something that I could do, and even that bitch Margo thinks I'm pretty. She says I'm as pretty as some of the women on television.

And Daddy always sees to it that I wear good clothes and have my hair done and wear a lot of makeup and things. I'd rather look like the girls my age, but Daddy insists I do it his way. At school nobody talks to me, except sometimes to call me a whore or rich bitch. Well, I don't like them either, and that's why I have to run away.

Love, Debra

June 22

Dear Mom,
I'm writing this from a drive-in on my way to Chicago. I waited for Daddy and Margo to go off to work. (Margo isn't a waitress anymore. She works in Daddy's office at the lumber company.) I didn't drive to school. Instead I have this map I'm following down to Chicago.

You know, of course, that I'm too young to drive, but that doesn't make any difference in our town where anything Daddy wants he gets. I always drive carefully, so I've never been stopped for anything, and Dad only lets me drive back and forth to school, so it's always been pretty safe. But the police wouldn't dare do anything to me here.

I know it has to be different away from town, but I look more like 21 than 15, and I'm driving very very carefully.

Anyway, this drive-in is just across from Wisconsin in Illinois, and I'm eating a hamburger and another strawberry shake just for you.

I don't think I have to worry about money for awhile because I had a couple hundred of my own, and I took $1000 out of Daddy's dresser before I left. I also left him and Margo a note that I've run away in the Cadillac. I don't think they'll be too worried. They always like to get me out of their hair. I hope they don't try to get me back, because I'm not going. This is better for everybody. I'll be in Chicago soon, and then I'll get a waitress job. It has to be in a restaurant where they don't serve drinks, because I hate drinking so much. As much as I loved you, Mom, I always hated your drinking and all the pills you took, so I'll never do that. You were always a good mom when you weren't drinking, but when you were, you were as bad as Daddy. You never cared about me at all when you were drinking.

I packed all my nice clothes so I can get a good job, but I've just spilled my strawberry milkshake on my nice white dress and I'm glad. I'll wear it as long as I can with the milkshake stain on it. Daddy would be furious.

I would like to say that I'm happy about what I'm doing, but I'm not. I'm very lonely and scared out here at the drive-in, thinking about what I'm doing. But I'd be scared and lonely at home too, so this is all right.

Whenever I need somebody to talk to, I'll write you a letter. If there's a Heaven, you'll be reading it.

Love, Debra

P.S. Mom, it's occurred to me that you might be receiving these letters even though I don't know where to send them. So of course I've also felt you might be able to answer them somehow, even if that does seem crazy, even to me, your crazy daughter.

So I thought I'd ask the question, Mom, just where are you? Where did Dad have you put away after you died? Is it true what Dad told me, that you never wanted to let me know where you are?

There are two cemeteries in town that I know of. I suppose if Dad had you buried in one of them, it would be the one on the East Side where the wealthy are put away, but maybe to fool me he had you buried on the West Side. Of course, maybe he had you cremated. (I think that's what I'll choose if I ever have the choice. There's something nice about being thrown in the wind to fly like a bird.) But maybe you wanted to be cut up and put in bottles for science. I hope that's not what happened, because if I ever get back to school and take biology again, I don't want to think that I'm dissecting my own mother. I mean, some things are too sick even for your sick daughter.

June 23

Dear Mom,

I got to the city at last and it's pretty scary. Chicago is too big, and everybody who drives is a maniac. They honk and yell at each other and give each other the finger while going as fast as they can, running red lights, cutting each other off. Driving in Chicago is like being in the school playground in grade school, except the kids used to have fun. In Chicago the drivers just hate each other.

So I was really upset by the time I found Lincoln Park and left my car by the zoo. I didn't know how hungry I was until I found a restaurant near the park and had a big spaghetti dinner. I also had a salad, Mom, not because I like them but because you always wanted me to eat a salad.

Then I went back to the zoo and saw all the animals. Lincoln Park Zoo is the best I've ever been to. I like it better than Milwaukee. The animals are a lot nicer than Chicago drivers. Actually, animals, from the way I see it, are just nicer than people anyway. That doesn't mean that I'd get in the tiger cage, because he'd eat me, but at least the tiger is nice to other tigers. At home I never found very many people who were nice to me.

So I walked around and saw the elephant and the zebra

and the giraffe, of course, and all the birds in the birdhouse, just about everything until I got to the monkey house, and that's when I got sad, Mom, because they were just like me, swinging from their tails, jumping around and making a lot of noise, doing everything to get the people to love them, but all the time they have to stay in the cages. It was like me at home, always having to look pretty to please Dad, but I could never get out to be myself. Maybe that's why nobody liked me, because I was always fake and on exhibit.

Now I know that these animals would like to get out of their cages and escape like me. Of course, they don't have a Cadillac to escape in, and they don't have a thousand dollars to take from their dads.

I always carry my money with me, Mom, because I don't want to lose it. It's beginning to get late, and maybe I'll go back to that restaurant to have a hamburger this time, and then I'll go back to sleep in my car. I could find a motel or something, but I want to sleep with the animals, because I like to hear them talking to each other. I haven't been able to talk to anybody in Chicago, just like I couldn't talk to anybody at home, but I talked a lot to the animals, and I like to hear them when they use their language.

Also, Mom, the monkeys and the apes and the orangutans, chimpanzees, all of them at the monkey house, really seem to love their kids. I watched for a long time this little mom monkey carrying and feeding her little baby. The baby jumped around and swung off the bars and ropes just like she did. Maybe I was the baby and you were the mom before you drank too much. I bet you caught me a lot when I was running around and getting into things. And then you held me and fed me just like the mommy monkey does.

I hope you're happier in Heaven than you were down here.

Love, Debra

6

June 25

Dear Mom,
Sleeping in the park was no fun. The car was cold, and once I heard somebody outside and they tried to get in. Thank goodness I had all the doors locked, but I lay real still so the person wouldn't know I was inside. After that, I couldn't really get to sleep, even though it was nice to hear the birds and animals talking in the zoo.

So as soon as it got light, I went back to my restaurant for breakfast. It's a nice restaurant and maybe I'll try to get a waitress job there, as soon as I find a place to live.

Anyway, I knew I was looking a little bad after a full day of driving and sleeping in the car, when the waitress started talking to me. She's young and pretty and her name is Joan. She seemed to know that I'd just arrived in town and wanted to know more about me. So she sat at my table for awhile when I was eating, and I learned that she grew up in a town called Mattoon on the Mississippi River and came to Chicago with a boyfriend a few years ago. After her boyfriend ran away she started waiting tables, and this is her fifth job in two years. She told me I could always get myself a waitress job to get by in Chicago.

Then she told me to go to the washroom downstairs to wash up and put on my makeup before sending me to her hotel not far away on LaSalle St. So, Mom, I got my first place to live in Chicago, a little room at the Farling Hotel with my own sink and bathroom and plenty of roaches, all for just $40 a week. Joan lives in the hotel too. She told me it gets a little wild at times, but I don't have to worry about anything. Just call down to the desk if I have trouble, and she'll help me too.

So I've made my first friend in Chicago, which is one more than I have at home, and I know this is the right thing to do.

Anyway, the first thing I did when I got into my room was go to bed and sleep most of the day. So I guess I didn't get too much sleep in the car.

7

I was able to drive my stuff to the hotel, and Dan the desk clerk helped me get it all up to my room, but then I had a real hard time finding a place to park the Cadillac. Also I'll have to keep moving it, because there don't seem to be places in Chicago where you can leave a car for long. Maybe I'll have to find a garage to keep it. Anyway, I have a feeling my money won't last for long here. I'll have to start waiting tables pretty soon.

After I woke up I phoned Joan, who lives downstairs in room 252. I live in 338, if you ever care to contact me from Heaven (ha ha).

So Joan and I sat in the coffeehouse downstairs, and I had coffee with another hamburger. After awhile, Dan the desk clerk, he came and sat with us, and I learned that Dan and Joan live together.

Joan told me that I should always be friendly with the desk clerks because that way they'll protect me and do things for me, like see to it that only the right people are let up to see me in my room. She told me to watch out for a lot of bad characters in the hotel and around Chicago everywhere, because there are always people out to use a young pretty girl. I didn't know exactly what she meant, but when she said it, Dan laughed.

I don't think I like Dan much. He has bad teeth and is a little older than Joan who told me she's 20. Dan is skinny and he crouches all the time, and he smells of cigarettes that he can't stop smoking. He's from Chicago's West Side, and his father was a cop before being thrown off the police force. He didn't tell me why.

Joan said she came from a nice family in Mattoon where both her mother and father were teachers, and nobody ever took a drink or did much of anything. That's why she ran out here with her high school boyfriend, but he decided to go to the university in Champaign and left her. But that was okay because she didn't love him anyway, and she's had lots of boyfriends since then. Dan got angry when she talked about her boyfriends. I guess he's jealous.

8

I brushed my teeth when I got to my hotel room. I thought you'd like to know that, Mom, and I don't want you to get mad, but I've decided I don't want to wear the clothes Daddy bought for me. So I'm wearing a pair of jeans and a shirt Joan gave to me. I'm not going to use makeup either, except for a little lipstick maybe and some eyeshadow. And for the first time, Mom, I look like the girls back home.

Tomorrow I'll go back to the zoo and see if my animals like me better this way.

Love, Debra

June 28

Dear Mom,

I don't know about this getting close and trusting desk clerks like Joan told me to do, because I was in my room when somebody knocked on the door. I opened it expecting Joan, but it was Dan. I should have known from the dumb way he was smiling at me that I shouldn't have let him in, but I didn't have much choice because he had already pushed himself in before I could stop him.

Then he started to talk, and I didn't want to hear anything he said, like Joan being a slut and sleeping with everybody who ever asked, and how he was tired of it all. And then he said that he was really a pretty good man, and that he was going to get out of the hotel pimping game and settle down with a real job and get married and raise a family, as soon as the right person came along. I never had a chance to say a thing. It was my job to sit on the bed and look interested, which I was not, because I wanted him to leave so I could read my magazine. Also I found him a little scary.

Pretty soon I found out why. He got on the bed beside me, and I knew he was going to try something just like Dad, but he didn't know, when he touched me, just how hard I could scream. So he got away from me before everybody in the

9

hotel would have to come to see what was happening.

Then he got real apologetic, telling me how much he liked me but would do nothing to hurt me and please don't tell Joan any of this, because it was just a mistake that would never happen again.

Well, I walked right to the restaurant where Joan was then at work, and I told her everything that happened. She thanked me but was more amused, it seemed, than mad. She told me that Dan was always that way and he hit on every young woman who ever came to the hotel, and not to worry about him because she'd see him tonight and straighten him out about me.

But I didn't go back to the hotel, because I didn't want to see Dan again, not until Joan got off work and straightened him out anyway. I walked downtown to the public library instead. That's one thing I can like about Chicago, the public library. It's the biggest library I've ever been in, and I went to the place where I could sit and listen to records. I was able to sit all afternoon listening to The Who, because I hadn't heard them since I left home.

I also got to walk along the lake, and this nice boy talked to me. His name is Robert, and he's going to Taft High School in Chicago. He didn't want anything from me but to talk and joke around. He did some cartwheels and stood on a chess table to act like a king. He was very funny and we exchanged telephone numbers. Even if he never calls me and I never see him again, it was nice being with him by the lake.

When I got back to the hotel, Dan was working behind the desk and he acted like nothing ever happened. I got to wondering how much I could trust him not to let dangerous and bad people up to my room after what he tried today.

I was really happy when Joan got home from her restaurant job, but she also acted like nothing had happened. But she took me out to Wells St. a block away for a ham sandwich and a beer in this bar. I didn't like the beer, but I drank it anyway. Everybody there seemed to know Joan, and several men came up to talk to her. They even talked to me a little bit too, but none of them were fun like Robert.

Love, Debra

                                                              July 3
Dear Mom,
I guess we don't have to worry about the Cadillac anymore. It's gone. For a week, I did nothing but drive Joan and her friends everywhere, and it's probably a good thing that it's gone, because my $1000 is already down to several hundred because of paying for the gas. But Joan had me drive all around Chicago to visit her friends and go to these wild parties. I wasn't wild, but Joan certainly was. I think she's slept with every man in Chicago. Now I know why Dan gets mad at her sometimes. And everybody but me drinks and drugs too much. There was a lot of that back home too, but I was never in on it and I'm not in on it now.

Anyway, I was getting tired of trying to find parking places, but now I don't have to worry about it because I parked it on Schiller one night and the next morning it wasn't there. Maybe one of Joan's creepy friends took it, I don't know. Joan has some nice friends who seem to like me, but she has some others who are just bad, and everybody's into drinking and drugging all the time.

At first I thought I'd report the missing car to the police, but then they'd find out that I'm underage to have a car and don't have a legal license. They'd also find out that I'm a runaway and send me back to Wisconsin. I'm not ready to go home yet.

And if Dad wants another Cadillac, he can just buy one.

Another thing, Mom, I want to assure you I've been good about the booze and drugs. And I haven't had trouble telling the men I don't want to sleep with them. I have smoked a little pot, but I got so scared after that, thinking everybody in

11

my room wanted to hurt me or even kill me, that I won't do it anymore. And after passing up coke for days, I did sniff up a line, but all it did for me was make me sick. (Puking seems to be a way of life with the people here. The maid has to clean up my bathroom almost every day and sometimes the rug in my sleeping room too.)

I hate the idea of drinking, as you know, after what it did to you, but I bought some vanilla ice cream at Walgreen's, and Joan insisted on pouring muscatel on it. This will surprise you, Mom, but that makes an excellent sundae, and I've never felt better eating ice cream. So for several days in a row, Joan and I got high on muscatel sundaes, but it's nothing to worry about, because even with muscatel on it there's only so much ice cream you can eat.

Love, Debra

July 5

Dear Mom,

The nicest thing happened to me. I was walking through Lincoln Park and met Robert again. You know, the boy from Taft High School who does all the funny things?

Well, Robert wasn't feeling all that good this time. He was dirty and had been living in Lincoln Park for 3 days because his mother threw him out of their house. He told me it was because he didn't have a job and his father's been dead a long time now and his mother couldn't afford to keep him any longer.

I told him I didn't know what to do, and he said that it's happened before, and he always knew how to survive. He goes to the gay bars on Wells St., he told me, and lets the faggots pick him up, and sometimes he finds a faggot to keep him for a few weeks, but he can never manage it longer than that because he hates them so.

12

Some aren't bad people, he told me, but he wanted to kill them for what they made him do with his body. I told him he didn't have to do that yet because he could stay with me in my hotel.

So we went there, and Mom, it's different from doing it with Daddy, because I really like Robert and he's a kid like me. He's very gentle, not like Dad. He tells me he knows how to do everything, because he's had a lot of experience. So for two solid days and nights we hardly even got out of bed. Robert used up six condoms, but then neither of us wanted to go out for more, but I don't think we have to worry because I just started my period. Robert said he didn't mind making love to me with my period because it just made it better. And I didn't have to do any of the things that Daddy made me do to hurt me.

I think I'm in love with him, Mom. He's really pretty skinny like Dan, and he isn't even as big as Dan, but he has this cute red hair and freckles. He tells me he's 16, but I find that hard to believe.

Anyway, he ate up everything in my little fridge, all my peanut butter and crackers and cream cheese and even my ice cream with all my muscatel. (What he didn't put on the ice cream he just drank out of the bottle.) He told me he hadn't eaten in a couple days. So when we finally got out of bed I took him out to eat some more in a restaurant.

He tells me not to worry when the money runs out, be-cause he can always get us some more at the gay bars. I asked him how he could do so well when he was so dirty and raggedy. He told me that the fags like it that way because then they can clean him up and buy him nice clothes. Faggots like to buy nice clothes, he told me.

Since this is the first boy I ever loved and the first person my own age I ever had sex with, I'll have to be careful, Mom, because I think I want him too much—especially since he keeps talking about how we'll get married and have a house on the West Side where he grew up, and we'll have kids too, but he won't just die like his dad and leave me to raise them somehow.

Another thing about Robert, he didn't light up a roach or bring out his fixings or snort a line of coke the first thing when he got in my room. I say this because that's what all Joan's friends do. Robert did drink up all my muscatel, but he didn't seem to be desperate for anything, except me, of course, but that's because he loves me as much as I love him.

Love, Debra

July 6

Dear Mom,

Robert took me to this strangest coffeehouse on Wells St., about a block from our hotel. It's called the Foundry, because it's where God does his work beating the metal of humanity into moral shape. It used to be called the Flow, because it was where you got in the holy flow with God.

And it's also a commune for all these men and women and kids to live, and they all wear blue uniforms like a bunch of little airline pilots, and they all wear these giant crosses around their necks, dwarfing those things the Catholics wear around theirs.

Anyway, it's a pretty nice coffeehouse upstairs above an expensive restaurant, so you think you're entering real class, but it's really pretty simple when you get up there. They only serve coffee and tea and a few sandwiches, but they attract a whole bunch of interesting people, like the musicians and the actors from Second City, and everything from runaway kids like me to businessmen.

Then the uniformed people, who are all pretty nice, serve you and sit with you and talk. Sometimes they try to make you a member of the Foundry by pushing their literature about worshipping Lucifer and things, but sometimes they just talk about your life and problems, and they'll help you get housing if you need it, or they'll help you search for employment and tell you where to find free food, things like that.

It's funny, because at the same time they'll be helping some frightened mother with two small kids who's just rolled in from Kansas and has no money and no place to live, hookers and drug dealers will be working the coffeehouse, and once Sister Mehitabel was caught doing sex acts with this creep named Ted in the kitchen.

The reason they're the Foundry now when they used to be the Flow is that everybody with the blue uniforms is supposed to be celibate unless you get married to somebody else in a blue uniform (which happens with everybody sitting in a circle with incense all over and a weird ceremony with one of the fathers dancing all around inside the circle making strange noises while Father Whaleblub plays ridiculous music on his guitar that he himself composed) but the founder of this movement is a Christlike creature whose picture used to be all over the walls. His name is Father de Goebels, and Father de Goebels, who is married to Mother Jehoshaphat, was caught in bed with Sister Reunion.

Overnight, Father de Goebels' pictures came off the wall and the Flow became the Foundry, but de Goebels kept almost half of his people to flow off to the other side of town to open another coffeehouse and become the Current.

All this information I got talking to people in the Foundry Coffeehouse, but none of this information comes from the uniformed people because they just say they had a difference in religion. But one person who can tell everything is Laura, because Laura used to be Sister Twinklestar before she gave it all up to go back into prostitution.

Anyway, Robert likes to go to the coffeehouse because he will do anything not to go back to the gay bars, and at the coffeehouse he can sell dope, and it's a good thing too, because my money is almost completely gone. Robert's going to have to pay my weekly hotel bill next time.

Love, Debra

July 10

Dear Mom,
One of my friends at the hotel is Richard the night desk clerk. Sometimes when I can't sleep, I go downstairs and talk to him. He's 50 years old, short and stocky and bent like a small ape, with a big red beard. I think he looks at me like a daughter. I kind of like this because Dad never treated me like that, as you know. Also when I want to get away from Robert and Joan and everybody else, I can go to Richard's room and he always gives me hot chocolate or a Coke. He never tries to turn me on with drugs or get me to drink wine like the others do.

I've learned that I can tell Richard everything. He tells me that Robert is okay but watch out for Joan and Dan. Joan's okay, he says, but she'll do anything that Dan has a mind to.

I told him how I ran away from home in Wisconsin, and he says I'm probably better off living in the Farling Hotel than a lot of places. The other day he even bought me a teddybear. I don't know when the last time is that somebody gave me one. You and Daddy were always too busy trying to make me act adult to give me dolls and teddybears.

Anyway, Richard tells me he's an old wino. He used to be a jazz musician and has played with people like Brubeck and Dizzy Gillespie. He's even written some music that they played. But he got in trouble with booze and lost everything. Then after spending 10 years on skid row, he got tired and went to a place called Chicago Alcoholic Treatment Center, and now he goes to Alcoholics Anonymous. He thinks just about everybody in the hotel could use AA or NA, which is

16

Narcotics Anonymous, and if I keep hanging around Dan and Joan, I will too.

Richard goes to the Foundry too. He has coffee and talks to the sisters and they try to get him to join and become one of the brothers. He isn't about to do it, but he does handle their soup line, which means he makes soup in a big pot and gets it on a truck, then he and one of the brothers or sisters takes it to Madison St. to serve to the winos.

I went with him once and it's pretty funny, because we set up in front of a flop called the Star Hotel run by the Episcopal Church, and most of the men who came to us for a cup of our soup cursed us and told us where we could shove our soup. Richard just cursed back at them. They could eat our soup or else. Some of the winos were polite and thanked us, but many told us we had the worst soup on the street, and one old wino whipped out his penis and tried to piss in the soup. Richard chased him into the Star Hotel.

Madison St. is kind of strange because most of it is torn down, at least the skid row part. Richard tells me the scene has moved to Wilson Ave. now.

Usually after Richard gets done returning the truck and washing out the big soup kettle, he has to get to an AA meeting to settle down. He says that no ex-wino should get close to practicing winos because it's too much of a tempta-tion to join them. I certainly don't know what for!

Anyway, Mom, all my money is gone. It only took 3 weeks. I don't know where it went but I'm sure that Robert and Joan helped themselves to a lot, especially when they wanted some drugs. I didn't mind. I was just happy to help them out.

I went to a couple of places on Wells St. and asked them if I could waitress for them, but they wanted someone with experience and they didn't believe me when I lied about my age.

Robert, as you know, said that he'd take care of me with the money he makes selling dope, but now I see how much of my money he's taken, so it looks like that won't work out.

17

If I thought that you could send me money from Heaven, I'd ask, because I know you'd send it to me. But I know I can't ask Dad. He'd just get the police to send me home and I know he doesn't want me anyway, so why bother?

Richard doesn't seem to understand this. He won't give me money because he thinks it would just go to my friends for their drugs, like most of the money I had did. He thinks I should contact Dad and is more than willing to put through the call when I'm ready. Of course Richard wouldn't have any money anyway, not working as desk clerk of the Farling Hotel.

Love, Debra

July 17

Dear Mom,

I had no money, and that was pretty scary. Richard fed me a few times, and Robert took me out once, but it got so I couldn't even afford toothpaste. So I was sitting in my room crying when Joan came in to comfort me. I told her that I couldn't even find waitress work, and she said not to worry because she could do a lot better for me. First she suggested that I sniff some coke because it would make me feel stronger. I told her that the only time I'd sniffed it, I'd gotten sick, but she told me that it happens that way a lot the first time. So I sniffed a line, and she was right. All my problems went away, and I knew I was in control. So I asked Joan what I should do.

She told me to dress up and put my makeup on just like Dad used to make me do, then go to the Foundry Coffeehouse and wait, because she knew this man named Jeffrey who was just waiting for a chance to get at me. I asked her what that meant, because I knew Jeffrey. He came to the coffeehouse a lot and was the head of some department at the shoe factory on Wells St. Joan just winked and said I knew what she meant. She said she'd go talk to Jeffrey, and he'd meet me at the coffeehouse and take me back to my hotel room. I'd have sex with him and he'd give me $50 for it.

Well, Mom, $50 is a lot of money when you're broke, so I decided to do it. I just hoped that Robert wouldn't find out. I didn't want Richard to know either, because I knew he wouldn't approve. Also it was kind of exciting to think that a nice businessman like Jeffrey might want to love me.

So I got dressed up like Joan told me to. She watched me do it and laughed, because she told me I looked just right for the part. Then we went to the coffeehouse and Joan went down the street to find Jeffrey at the shoe factory.

I almost never wear anything but jeans and a shirt since Joan first got me to wear hers and I went off to the Gap to get some jeans and shirts of my own, so I was surprised when I went to the Foundry Coffeehouse all dressed up like the hookers in there that nobody came to me and said a thing.

Sister Nell just brought me a cup of coffee and asked me how things were at the hotel. When I told her I'd run out of money, she just laughed and winked, like she knew exactly what I was doing and it didn't make any difference. This was real strange to me, Mom, because Sister Nell and all the others had been talking to me recently about becoming a sister myself at the Foundry, and now I was about to be a hooker for $50 and nobody seemed much to care.

Well, I waited for awhile, talking to Sister Nell and some of my friends. There were two other hookers there too, waiting for what might show up. One, named Lulu, asked me who I was waiting for, and I told her Jeffrey. She told me that was good because Jeffrey was a nice man and would probably be good for $75 if I'd just do what he wanted. I wondered what that might be.

Anyway, Jeffrey came into the coffeehouse with Joan. Then Joan smiled and nodded to me slyly, and Jeffrey came up to me himself and asked if I'd like to go out. On the way out, Jeffrey handed Sister Nell a $10 bill for the Foundry.

We didn't go to my hotel. Instead Jeffrey got us a cab to

his loft on Sedgewick St. in Old Town. It was a beautiful place with nice modern furniture and paintings all over the walls that Jeffrey said he'd purchased from local painters to help them out. He took out a wad of bills and shoved them into my purse as we sat on a big sofa. Then he told me to take off my clothes, and while I did he made us some drinks. I knew I wouldn't drink mine but I'd pretend, to please Jeffrey. After all, he was paying for it. He told me to keep my high-heeled shoes on, which I thought was a little weird, but he said he liked that.

Then I sat on the sofa and he sat in a chair in front of me so he could look at me. He told me I was lucky to be so pretty and have a body like that, but all he did was look at me and ask me about myself. Then after I'd told him all about you and Daddy and horrible Wisconsin where nobody liked me and how I ran away, he started talking about himself and how he'd grown up in Chicago and had his MBA from the University of Chicago and how he'd already been married three times and wasn't quite 30 years old yet, so he guessed marriage wasn't for him even though he liked pretty girls, and I was one of the prettiest.

He asked me if I'd been doing this for long, and I told him I'd just run out of money and this was the first time. At first he laughed like this had to be impossible, but later he told me he believed me. He told me not to worry because he was always very gentle and wouldn't even be doing this if he didn't like me. Of course I knew this was a lie, after talking to the hooker at the coffeehouse, and I suspected Jeffrey had a lot of us girls in his apartment. But I also liked him, and it was nice to hear nice things about myself, because Robert doesn't know how to say the things to make a girl feel good.

He asked me if I was cold, and of course I was, with the goosebumps all over me, so he sat down on the sofa beside me and held me. I wondered why he didn't take off his own clothes, but who was I to ask?

Anyway, he had a few more drinks and asked me why I didn't finish mine. I told him I didn't like liquor. So he asked me if I'd like some coke, and I said yes, so we sniffed some coke and that made me feel great to be high with a man like Jeffrey.

I don't know how long we were there, but Jeffrey cooked us this great gourmet dinner of chicken breasts and some kind of cream sauce. Since I was cold I stood next to the oven, and Jeffrey put some of the cream sauce on my nipples to lick it off, which is the first time he even touched me, except to hold me when I was cold.

Then after dinner Jeffrey went away long enough to come back in his robe, and sometimes it would part and open at his groin because his thing was hard.

But then he did something that surprised me. He told me to put my clothes back on, and only then did he kiss me for the first time, and I don't think I've ever loved a man more. He told me again that I was pretty, maybe the prettiest girl he's had for a long time, and he asked me if I'd see him at the coffeehouse again tomorrow at the same time. I told him I would, and he asked me to wear the very same clothes again. (I don't know why that made a difference, Mom, since I was naked except for my shoes all the time I was there.)

Anyway, I hurried back to my hotel because I wanted to find Robert and get in bed with him, because I was really horny, and in my purse I found 10 $10 bills. I could pay my hotel bill and still have a lot left over.

Love, Debra

21

July 18

Dear Mom,

I'm writing this letter a day after the one before this to assure
you that Jeffrey is not the love of my life like I thought he
might be yesterday.

Of course I told Robert what I had done, and he was
pleased about the $100 but I could tell he wasn't too happy
that I'd paraded around nude for Jeffrey and even less happy
that I went back to see him again today.

But this time it was different. Jeffrey picked me up at the
Foundry Coffeehouse again and took me to his apartment, but
another man was waiting there for us, a big fat man named
Larry who stank of booze and cigars, even worse than Dan
stinks.

Jeffrey put the money in my purse, so I had to take off my
clothes again, but this Larry was not nice like Jeffrey had
been. He called me dirty names like teenaged whore and
nubile dragon. He laughed when I asked him what a nubile
dragon is and told me it's a young slut like myself. Jeffrey
just sat there and watched everything.

They asked me if I wanted to shoot up with them and I
told them no, until Jeffrey assured me that I'd like it and had
to do it for the money he was paying me. So I let Larry stab
me in my fanny with a needle, after feeling all over it with his
big hand when I bent over, and I felt very relaxed and happy
then.

They then took me into the bedroom and Larry took off all
his clothes as I lay on the bed. Jeffrey had his camera to take
pictures. I not only felt relaxed and happy but I didn't care
about anything by then, so I didn't mind when fat Larry got
on the bed with me.

Larry took his time with me, making me do all the things
Dad used to make me do. Even though I didn't really feel
anything, I could see Larry get uptight when I acted that way
and since I didn't want him to hurt me I started to pretend that
I liked what we were doing.

22

And I learned something, Mom, something I've known for a long time really, and that's how not to be there. When I was bending over his fat belly to kiss his penis, I just got out of myself to observe the whole silly business from a seat on the side of the bed. I almost wanted to laugh, because that dumb Larry thought he was really exciting me when I couldn't really feel a thing. If he'd strangled me it wouldn't have made that much difference.

I wasn't there very long this time. As soon as Larry came all over my belly (which made him mad, because he wanted to come inside me, or so he said) he just told me to get dressed and get out. All Jeffrey was doing all this time was taking pictures, and he didn't say a thing when I went back into the living room and put on my clothes.

By the time I was ready to say good-bye, Jeffrey and Larry were well on their way to getting drunk and all Jeffrey did was point toward the door because they were too busy discussing the Cubs by then.

I walked out down to the street and must admit I felt pleased to think that it could all be so easy. Of course, I knew that shot that Larry gave me helped, and I was still high when I reached into my purse to count my money. That disappointed me because it was only $50 this time. Still $150 for two days of labor like this, especially the second day which took less than an hour, is pretty good money.

So I walked back to the hotel and found Robert lying face down on our bed. I told him of our good luck about the $150, but when he unburied his head from the pillow I could see that he was crying. He said that I was just like all the others, and that he'd never marry me now. He told me that all the things Larry called me were true.

I tried to explain to him that none of this meant anything, because I might just as well have not been there, and the only thing that was important was the $150. It took Joan to convince him. She told him the same thing I had, but she explained it a little better. She said that Jeffrey and Larry were

23

just johns and had really been taken for $150, because I hadn't given them anything really but a little play-acting and make-believe. What was worth $150 to them wasn't worth a penny to me, but still I got the $150 out of it, almost like I'd robbed them. Robert kind of liked that, and later, when we made love, I kept telling him that he's the only one, and he believed it.

Actually, I can take or leave Robert, but it was still good to make peace.

When I told Richard what I'd done, he just asked if I'd been hurt. I told him no and paid my hotel bill. Later he said that he'd like me to go back home to Wisconsin, but I can't do that, Mom, as you know.

Love, Debra

August 1

Dear Mom,

I guess things have gotten a lot better with me, because I have all the money I need and more. Joan told me a few things about the profession, because it turns out that she's done a lot of hooking herself, when she tires of waitressing or just needs some extra money.

I certainly don't sit in the Foundry Coffeehouse anymore and wait for people like Jeffrey, because I do much better in a couple bars along Wells St. The bartenders know what I'm there for, and they help me get the right johns. All I have to do is tip them good. And some of the bartenders are really good friends of mine.

One of the bars is the Old Town Alehouse, but I don't hook there because I want one place I can just go to relax, and Timmy Light the bartender is my friend. He's in his 40's and he takes care of me like a father, but once, after closing the Alehouse at 2:00 a.m., Timmy took me upstairs and we slept together among the boxes. He knows I'm only 15, but he said that he liked it. But maybe the reason I trust Richard a little more is that Richard really doesn't want to sleep with me. It's nice to know at least one man I can be friends with without having to ball.

Anyway, I can hang out in these bars on Wells St., and for no more than sitting on a stool to talk or shooting some pool, I get these men to take me to their hotels or offices, sometimes even their homes, and I charge $50 but they usually give me more. I seldom spend more than a half hour with any of them, so I can make anywhere from $200 to $500 a day, and once I hooked up with a rich old drunk who gave me $1000.

Still I never seem to have much money, because I keep giving some to Robert or Joan. The only person in my hotel who has never asked for any was Richard. When I told Richard what was happening with my money, he took me to the First National Bank of Chicago and got me to open a checking account. I now have over a thousand in my account because Richard keeps pushing me to put more and more in it, before I spend it or give it away.

Robert is still my friend but we aren't as close as we used to be. He says he doesn't mind my hooking, but that's because he's fallen in love with Sister Hazel at the Foundry. Maybe I'd rather be Sister Hazel, because she gets all the attention now. Robert wouldn't care about me at all, I bet, if I weren't giving him money and a place to stay. Of course he spends a lot of nights away now, I suppose with Sister Hazel.

Even Joan is more distant than she used to be. I think she and Dan don't want me around except when they need money for their dope.

So my best friends now are in the bars, and they're usually the bartenders. If not the bartenders, I guess I'm friends with some of my johns who keep coming back. They'll give me money and tell me how to live my life. Some don't even care much about the sex, or that's how it seems, but they're as lonely as I am and we'll talk for hours about their families and their problems, and with some I can talk about you and

Daddy and horrible Wisconsin and life at the Farling Hotel.
They like it when I tell them about me, because then they can
play daddy.

But even then I feel empty, Mom, because they always
leave, or I always leave, after they give me the money, and I
know they're going home to their families or loved ones and
I'm going back to the bars to find another daddy.

You'd think I'd be happy with all the money I'm making,
but some days it's all I can do to start working, and every
night when I get done I'm erased and lonely again, so what's
the use?

If it weren't for Richard I might not make it. I might just
take all the pills and drink all the booze I can find and then
maybe I wouldn't have to wake up in the morning. This hotel
is famous for that. I've only been here 5 weeks and already
there have been two women found dead in the morning and
removed by the police in plastic bags on stretchers.

Richard tells me this helps keep him sober, because almost
all of the deaths at the Farling are caused by drugs and booze.
He sees more of it than anybody else since he works at night
when most of it goes on. He'll say goodnight to what seems
like a perfectly healthy person and the next morning watch
her carried out dead, usually from an overdose, but one
woman got beaten to death by a drunken boyfriend while her
2 year old son had to stand by and watch. She screamed and
screamed but nobody in nearby rooms did a thing, not even
phoning Richard to tell him about it.

The healthiest people at the Farling seem to be the old
people on retirement or social security. They have a society
among themselves that centers in the lobby or the restaurant.
Everybody else is a boozer or druggy or near psychotic of
some kind, with a handful of pimps and hookers like me. But
some of those hookers have been doing it for years, and
they're too far gone, Richard says, to consider another way of
life. Honest, Mom, that will never happen to me. I'll meet
some man in one of the Wells St. bars, or the Alehouse
maybe, and he'll love me and get me out of this.

26

Right now I get relief by drinking a little and doing drugs. I have to watch out for the coke, I know it can get me in trouble. But I kind of like goofballs because then it doesn't really matter what I'm doing, because I can't feel anything and don't care.

This is important, Mom, because I see all these horrible things, like one man was knifed to death right in front of me when I was looking out the window of the Crystal Pistol on Wells St., and I saw a woman nearly beaten to death in another bar, and I've seen little kids crying and neglected with their parents passed out drunk on the bar. Once I just took this baby out of her mother's arms and gave her a bottle. The woman didn't even thank me when she woke up. She called me a whore and snatched her baby back.

When I really get depressed by all this I just walk up Wells to Lincoln Ave. If Joan's waitressing and if it's not too crowded, she'll spend some time with me calming me down. Also, I go back to the zoo a lot to see my animals.

My favorites are still in the monkey house. I like the baboons with the striped colors on their noses and bottoms best. But what I really like is how they treat their babies, carrying them around and feeding them, licking them and giving them affection. It makes me want to be a baby baboon, but I guess I'll have to make do with what I have.

Love, Debra

August 4

Dear Mom,

I at last had my first really bad experience hooking.

This man sat beside me at the Second Chance, and maybe it never would have happened if I'd been a little more sober, but it was late in the afternoon and I'd been there too long. Sometimes when that happens I just go to the hotel and sleep it off for awhile, but before I decided to do this, the man I mentioned sat down next to me.

He looked like a lot of middle aged men, a businessman type in a plaid sport jacket and dark pants. He seemed nice enough, but I don't know what we were talking about because I was too far gone. Anyway, I asked him out and we left the bar. I recall getting in the cab with him and then we were in his room. Even drunk I knew this wasn't much better than the Farling Hotel.

I started to take off my clothes and he hit me, knocking me down at the foot of the bed. Then he kicked me and told me to get up. I think I was completely sober by then.

He told me to lie down on the bed and I saw the knife he was holding. Well, almost from the beginning Joan had told me to carry mace in case of something like this, and maybe it was because I was drunk, but I'd taken off my skirt and panties but was still wearing my jacket, and that was good because in my jacket pocket was the mace.

So as soon as he glanced away I got the can out and let him have it right in the face. I had never used it before, so I didn't know how well it would work, but down he went gagging and writhing. I sprayed him again and smashed his head with the table lamp. I started to run out of there, but didn't want to leave with nothing. So I held the mace in one hand in case he woke up and took his wallet out of his pocket. I later counted the money I took, over $200.

Anyway, Mom, I almost ran out of there before I put on my panties and skirt. Just before I left I saw him move a little, and that was good, because I was afraid that I'd killed him.

When I left and ran down some stairs into a lobby and out

into the street, I saw that I'd just left a hotel on Clark St. across from Bughouse Square so I was able to catch a cab to the Farling not too far away. It wasn't until I got back up in my room that the terror hit me and I kneeled before my toilet to vomit for half an hour. Then I had this terrific headache and lay down shaking with a couple aspirin in me. But I was too scared to stay there.

I went down to the desk, and Dan was on duty. I still didn't like him but I was happy he was there, and sat in the office without leaving, even to go to the bathroom, until Richard came on duty at 11:30.

"You look terrible," he said to me.

"No kidding," I managed, and told him everything that had happened. I had told Dan everything too, but Dan had just laughed and said I needed a good pimp.

Richard didn't laugh. He got a little angry instead. "Look," he said, "you still don't know what you're doing, and you'll probably be killed before you learn. Are you sure you can't reconcile with your dad and go back home?"

Richard was getting boring, always telling me to go back home. You know, Mom, why I can't do that.

Anyway, about 3:00 a.m. I asked Richard if I could sleep in his room, and he said yes, because I just felt too scared to sleep in my own bed where it would be too easy to find me, even though the man I maced probably had no idea where I lived.

So I stopped in at my room just long enough to get the teddybear Richard had bought me, and I went to Richard's room. He'd given me the key, so I let myself in where all the walls were lined with books and there were still boxes of books that had never been emptied.

I took off all my clothes and got in his bed and waited, too scared to sleep. A couple times I called down to the desk and talked to Richard, and he always tried to say the things to calm me down.

Around 8:00 Richard knocked on his door and I opened it, still lying in the bed. He said good morning and took off all his clothes. I was surprised to see that he didn't look at all like a 50 year old man. He was short and powerfully built with a big chest like some of the high school football players back home.

But when he got into bed beside me I didn't want to make love to him, because he'd be no better than a john and I felt this real hatred, like he was my father.

"Richard," I said, "please don't do it."

"Don't worry," he whispered, "I won't."

And as I held my teddybear, Richard held me, and I slept.

Love, Debra

August 5

Dear Mom,

Richard took me to a movie. You know I used to go to a lot of movies back home, all the movies I could get to because they were always better than the life I was living, but Richard is the first person to take me to a movie. Back home sometimes I'd find a boy in the movie, and we'd sit in back and neck (which I've never told you before this letter) but not you or Dad or anybody else ever actually took me to a movie.

We went to this matinee and when Richard was buying popcorn, the counter woman asked him if I was his daughter. That's when he put his arm around me and said yes. I can't tell you how good that made me feel. Anyway, the movie was "Panic at Needle Park" with Al Pacino and Kitty Winn, and I hated it because it was all about drugs in New York and I felt just like Kitty Winn who gets turned onto dope and hooking by Pacino.

It isn't that I hated it so much, but I wondered why Richard took me to it. I wondered if he wasn't telling me that I'm a bad girl and should straighten out. So I asked him if that's what he was doing and he just laughed, not taking it one bit

seriously, and said, "Yes, I'm going to turn you into a saint."
And that made me even madder, even if he did take me out
for an ice cream cone later.

Anyway, that night when Richard went to work I told him
that I didn't care to sleep in his bed but was going to sleep in
my own bed with Robert instead. He didn't seem to care, but
he gave me his key to get my teddybear from his room first.
This made me even madder because if Richard was going to
treat me so nicely, I guess he didn't care that I was mad.

I didn't expect to find Robert in my room because he
usually spent his nights with Sister Hazel someplace. But to
my disappointment, there indeed was Robert, lying on my bed
with a cigarette and a beer. He asked me where I'd been last
night, because he'd slept in my room then too.

I told him it was none of his business, and he got angry. So
I said, "What do you care? You're with Sister Hazel." So he
lied and said he'd never liked Sister Hazel as much as he likes
me, and he and Sister Hazel weren't seeing each other anymore because, in fact, he hates Sister Hazel who never did
anything but take drugs and talk about the wonderful Foundry
and how he too should get involved and become a brother.

I told him that I didn't care about either Sister Hazel or
him and that I wanted the key to my room back. Then he went
into his little boy hurt act, saying he never would have been
with Sister Hazel if he knew it would hurt our friendship.
This dumb conversation went on for hours, about Sister Hazel
and the key and how much he's always liked me, and of
course how terribly sorry he was.

Then he finally asked, "Where did you sleep last night?
You had a john?"

"No," I said happily, "I slept with Richard."

"That old crow of a night clerk!" he howled.

I giggled. "Have you ever seen that big chest of his? And
those big arms? He doesn't smell bad like you and Dan. I bet
he even takes a shower now and then."

"I don't smell like Dan!"

"You do now, sitting in this room doing nothing but drinking and smoking all the time."

"I could kill the old night clerk," he whimpered.

So we fought most of the night before finally getting in bed together. I didn't want to do anything with him, anymore than I had with Richard, so I just let him get turned on beside me and then I'd push him away to let me sleep. But I really couldn't sleep at all. Robert got to sleep before I did.

I was up, showered and dressed and munching potato chips before Robert awoke, and the first thing he asked is whether I'd been turning tricks and making much money, so I knew he wanted me to give him some. I asked why he didn't get some money from Sister Hazel, because she's been turning tricks. This really made him mad, so I told him how Sister Hazel had gone out with Jeffrey. This was a lie but I liked the way it made Robert scream and squirm.

It also made him get dressed pretty quick and leave, and I knew he was going to see Sister Hazel and get all this straightened out. But then I was alone, and sometimes I'm really frightened when I'm alone. I held my teddybear for a long time, but that didn't help enough.

So I went to Richard's room and he was just waking up, because it was already after noon. He asked me if I wanted to eat and he fixed me a breakfast of a couple soft boiled eggs and toast. It made me think of how you used to fix breakfast, Mom, just for you and me after Daddy had gone to work, but that was before you were drinking too much and I fixed the breakfasts.

Anyway, I told Richard everything that had happened with Robert, and he told me not to worry about it because that sort of thing usually turns out the way it should, even if it means never seeing Robert again. So he didn't tell me what to do and he didn't tell me I was bad. That's what I like about Richard, he doesn't judge me.

So after breakfast I felt too good to go to the bars. Instead I went to the zoo to talk to the monkeys and tell them about

32

Richard taking me to a movie and the woman asking if I was his daughter.

Love, Debra

Dear Mom,

I got to go on my first trip to New York. A friend of Joan's came to see me at her restaurant and he said he was putting together this troupe for a show in New York. It was to entertain clients in a convention.

He was getting together about 10 girls, maybe a few more, and he'd put us up in New York. Then we'd do what he called burlesque, which meant posing and dancing nude a little. And for this he'd pay us each $500.

Well, it all seemed a little crazy to me. I wondered why he couldn't just find his girls in New York. But as it turned out, everybody going to the convention was from Chicago.

So we all had a drunken party at the Hyatt and took a company plane to New York. I'm surprised we didn't all crash because of all the drinking and screwing around on the plane. We just kept high and switched partners all the way to New York and on to the Earth Hotel, right off Washington Square Park in the Village.

I think it was some kind of upholsterers convention, but I'm not sure. Our job was to stay in our suites in the hotel like some kind of harem, but I got tired of all this and took off for a walk through the Village.

I found myself on Christopher St. where most of the gays hang out, and after seeing all the pretty shops and restaurants and all the fun people seemed to be having, I wondered if I shouldn't be a lesbian, because I was becoming more and more dead inside from doing what I'd been doing.

I was getting sick of all the men, Mom, and trying to

pretend how much they pleased me while doing everything they wanted.

I think by now I'm drinking as much as I ever saw Daddy and you drink, but I can never handle it very well. I always pass out after a few drinks, unless I also sniff a little coke or take some speed. If I balance my drugs right I can stay awake for days and still be too high to feel anything, and that's the only way I can handle this life.

Anyway, at the end of Christopher St., I found Barrow St. Pier that extends way out into the Hudson, and beside it is moored this big ship that serves as the Maritime High School. I walked way to the end of the pier and saw all the couples holding hands and necking, and I started to cry because I was so lonely.

And pretty soon this young man sat next to me and asked what's the matter. When I told him, he said that he was Carry and he too was lonely, because he lived in Hoboken across the river and his girlfriend had just run away with another friend. Then he bought me an ice cream bar and we both ate ice cream while looking out at the big ships going up and down the Hudson. We even held hands, Mom, and this is what I always wanted from the boys at home.

So it really made me feel bad when we parted, Carry to return to Hoboken and me to the Earth Hotel. We exchanged telephone numbers and addresses, but I knew we'd never see each other again, with him in Hoboken and me in Chicago, but at least it was nice for a few hours.

I couldn't find my way back to the Earth, but a taxi took me there. I was sick and scared going back up to my suite. I didn't know how my disappearance would be taken. But I found everybody either involved in some kind of drunken sex act or else passed out.

So I just left the Earth again and found Cafe Borgia on Bleecker St., where I sat outside in the sun with my cafe mocha and watched the people walking through the village. Then I walked around Soho and went in and out of the galleries.

I got back to the Earth Hotel late at night and everybody
was passed out by then. So I took off my clothes and lay
down on a bed to sleep, and when people started to wake they
didn't even know I'd been gone. By the time we boarded the
plane for Chicago, everybody was pretty quiet and I may have
been the only one not totally wasted, me and maybe the pilot.

After they landed, the girls got paid off in the plane before
having to make our own way back into Chicago. They had
promised us $500 but of course they burned us with $100,
saying that we could get the rest at an address they gave us.
Later I tried to find the address, but it didn't exist.

I would have made a lot more money just staying on Wells
St., but at least I got my first trip to New York and I saw the
Village and held hands for awhile with that young man from
Hoboken.

Love, Debra

August 15

Dear Mom,
When I got back to the Farling, with all its dirt and roaches
and sick people, I really knew how much I hated it and
everything else in Chicago. I had enough in me to go to the
address our party leader had given us to collect my last $400,
and that's when I really crashed, knowing the address would
put me somewhere in the middle of Lake Michigan.

So I just stood on the Chicago Ave. beach and stared out
into the lake and cried. I've been crying a lot lately. Maybe
that's good, Mom, because as bad as it was at home, nobody
would ever let me cry. Well, the waves were pretty high off
the lake that morning and I thought, all I have to do is walk to
the end of the breakwater and if the waves haven't washed me
off by then, I can jump. They won't even know who I am
when they find me, so they'll just bury me someplace and that
will be it.

I even walked way out on that breakwater, Mom, but I got scared and thought maybe things would get better somehow. So I hurried back to the beach and sat playing in the sand. I'd make a sand castle right at the edge of the surf and when the water would come in, it would wash it all away, just like my life, nothing really going anyplace and everything that seemed to get started would kind of disappear.

I thought of Carry. So I walked back to the Farling and phoned him from my room. I guess I woke him. It was still pretty early in Chicago but a little later in Hoboken, NJ, I thought. Anyway, he didn't seem happy to hear from me and even suggested I never call him again because his girlfriend decided to get back with him and he didn't need other girls calling up just now. But we both agreed it was nice holding hands on the Barrow St. Pier, before we hung up.

Then I was really depressed. So I took my teddybear to Richard's room and he had just begun to sleep after working the desk all night, but he let me in. When I looked at him, a little too hairy and fat around the belly, with deep lines around his eyes and that bald spot on his head, he seemed very old to me. I knew that I wanted a young body like Carry's to hold.

But I got in bed and turned my back to Richard and held my teddybear. Richard did drape a big arm around me but then was quickly asleep. I just curled up with my teddybear and stared at the wall, just concentrating on this long crack that curved up over one of Richard's boxes of books. I was afraid to look away from that crack, because I knew it was the only thing holding me together at that point, that and Richard's arm pressing me into the mattress. Without them I would have come apart altogether, I was so scared.

Then I saw Dad sitting at the foot of my bed just looking at me, and I've never seen Dad look so pale and sad. I sat up and said hello. I told him that I was glad to see him because I loved and missed him. Part of this was even true, but the other part of me was just as scared of him as always. But he didn't answer, he just sat there staring, and the longer he stared the scareder I got. I asked him how he had found me, and still he didn't answer. So I reached over to wake up Richard, but Richard wasn't there. That's when I began to scream and Dad disappeared, he just wasn't there anymore.

There was a knock on the door and I opened it expecting to see Richard who maybe had forgotten his key, but it was old Mrs. McHenery from next door. She had heard the scream and wanted to see if everything was all right. Like I wrote earlier, the old people here are the nicest and sanest people in the hotel. I told her that everything was all right, and then she looked suspicious because I was sleeping in Richard's room. I couldn't much blame her.

Anyway, I had this strong urge to phone Dad for the first time. I hated to do it but still I had to. So I used Richard's phone and had the desk charge it to my phone and gave them the Wisconsin number.

Margo answered and that surprised me, because actually they both should have been off for work.

"What do you want?" she asked in her usual snotty way.

"Is Dad there?" I asked. "I'd like to talk to him."

There was this long pause before she said, "How did you know?"

"How do I know what?" I asked.

And then she talked nice for the first time. "Debra honey, your dad had an accident yesterday. His car had a collision on the Interstate."

I waited. "Well, what happened to him? Is he all right?"

"I'm afraid not, love. I'm afraid he was killed."

"Well, what should I do, Margo? Should I come home?"

She got snotty again. "Why should you do that? There's nothing you can do. You left and now he's dead, that's all. You don't have a home here anymore."

And she hung up.

So, Mom, I just held the telephone for a long time until Mr. Jenns, the hotel manager who always works the desk on the morning shift, told me to hang up.

I did and saw on Richard's alarm clock that it was already

2:00 p.m., which means that Richard had already gotten up and left, accounting for me being alone. I thought of Lake Michigan and wondered why I hadn't jumped off the end of the pier like I'd planned. And I saw a paring knife on Richard's table and wondered if it would be sharp enough to cut my throat or wrist. And then I got really scared thinking that's what I wanted to do, and I hardly had strength for anything by then. So I lay back down in Richard's bed and held my teddybear and stared at the crack in the wall. The longer I stared at it, the more I knew it was moving like a snake slowly twisting on the wall, and it seemed like it was coiling up and getting ready to strike me with its venomous fangs and crush me. I tried to move but I couldn't. All I could do was stare at the snake.

Thank god, Richard came back. At first he thought I was asleep, but then he saw my eyes popped open staring at the wall. He asked me what the matter was, but I couldn't speak. So he lay down on the bed beside me and tried to hold me. That didn't work, so forcefully he turned me toward him to hold me, but that put the snake behind me and I shrieked in terror. Richard asked what was the matter.

And I wailed, "The snake! The snake!"

It took awhile for Richard to figure it out and convince me that there was no snake. He put his fingers on the crack to prove it. But I was still scared, until he took his Chicagofest poster down from another wall to tape it over the crack.

Then I was able to tell him about my father being killed and my telephone call with Margo. He held me a long time while I cried and then took me out to breakfast at Joan's restaurant, where I told her everything. After that, Richard took me to the Art Institute to see all the paintings.

He really wanted to show me some pictures by Magritte and Francis Bacon because, according to Richard, they depicted the kind of nightmares I was having in his room. But I liked even better some paintings by Delacroix, because they were all full of action with lions eating horses and people fighting each other with swords and scimitars. I also liked a big pink woman holding her baby that Picasso did, because, Mom, I thought of how you must have held me when I was a baby.

Now that Daddy's dead, I guess I could write him letters too, but I'm afraid that his ghost would come visit me again. I'm as afraid of Daddy's ghost as I was of Daddy. At least there's nothing that can get me back to Wisconsin now.

After the Art Institute, Richard took me to dinner at Berghoff's, and that was very good because I've never had real German food before. I learned how good sauerkraut is when it's done right and isn't that sour stuff we used to eat out of the can. But what I liked best was the strudel for dessert, and Richard said he'd take me to the Red Star Inn sometime for the best apple pancakes. If I just keep Richard for a friend, I'll be fat soon.

We didn't get back to the hotel until Richard had to go on duty, and I sat in the office with him until almost 3:00, talking as he did the books. Then I went to bed in Richard's room again with my teddybear and I was glad that the poster covered up the crack because I've never been so tired.

Love, Debra

Dear Mom,

I had to get back to work, whether I liked it or not. Richard paid my rent one week but he said he couldn't do it two weeks in a row. So I loaded up on goofballs and hit the street again. But I'd only been at it a week, when I met this interesting man at the Foundry Coffeehouse. I think I told you that a lot of the local actors and artists come to the coffeehouse. Well, one of them is a bass player who accompanies some of the folk acts at the Earl of Old Town.

I find folk music boring. I guess it was great for your generation, but for me, if it's not rock I don't really care much for it. The bass player, Louie, works in the store of the Old Town School of Folk Music during the day and accompanies folk artists at night. Over the years, he's played behind people like Josh White, Theo Bikel, and Bob Gibson. I didn't know any of them, but I got to like going to the Earl just to be known as Louie's friend.

Well, Louie spent a few nights with me and I never took money from him, like I would from a john, because I like him. That's what I told him too, and he eventually said that he liked me too. And then he said that he didn't want me to hook anymore because he wanted me all to himself.

That's the first time I've found anybody like that. So right away I told Robert to get out and stay out. He wouldn't give me the key, but I got the desk clerks to know that I didn't want anything to do with him anymore, and then I got the word to Robert at the Foundry Coffeehouse that the police would be called if he ever went to the Farling Hotel again. At this, he gave me his key and said he wouldn't want any more to do with a slut like me anyway.

After that I learned that Robert had tested positive for AIDS but didn't know if he'd gotten it at the gay bars or from needles. It's then that I vowed never to share another needle with anybody.

Also, Mom, I should let you know that the girls in my profession only do safe sex now. It's probably safer doing it with most hookers around here than with girlfriends. Of course most of the girlfriends I know at the coffeehouse and on the street play around all the time. So if I get AIDS I bet everybody else around here does too.

Anyway let me tell you more about Louie. He's a 40 year old high school dropout who's never left Chicago except to play folk gigs all over the country. He even followed Steve Goodman down to Nashville a couple times. (Steve Goodman is a name I know. He died recently of leukemia, but all the folkies play his "City of New Orleans" song.)

Louie does something else too. He buys me flowers. Richard bought me flowers a couple times and also my teddybear, but it's more important when they come from Louie because Louie's just 40 and looks young, while Richard is 50 and more like a father.

Richard knows Louie and thinks he's a little lazy and dull but that I could do a good deal worse from the crop on Wells St.

Louie has also taken me to a movie. But what he likes to do best is play his bass or his guitar. Unlike most of the people I know who would rather talk about themselves all the time, Louie would just as soon not talk at all, because he's too busy either playing music himself or listening to it on his hi-fi. I just wish he'd listen to more rock and less country and folk.

So I've been spending less and less time at the hotel and more and more time at Louie's studio apartment in Old Town. What this usually means is lying around listening to music and smoking dope. Sometimes Louie's friends are there to lie around and smoke dope and listen to music with us. And we seem to live on pizza and potato chips, washed down by beer. It's no wonder that Louie's so fat and has so little energy except when he's playing the bass.

Then at night when Louie is not playing a gig himself, we'll go sit in at the Earl of Old Town. Last night we heard some character named U Utah Phillips. Louie says that he's great, but it's guys like U Utah Phillips that turn me onto the

41

Sex Pistols and Joan Jet. We heard John Prine not long ago, though, and he's pretty good. And we're always there to see Bob Gibson.

Anyway, if I keep living like this on pizza and potato chips, I'll get fat like Louie.

I guess I could just move in with him, but there really isn't enough room and I think I'd go crazy, Mom. Also, he talks about taking care of me, and in a sense he does, but I know I have to pay my own way because he barely makes enough money to get by for himself.

So I still work the street a little bit, just to pay my hotel bill and get by. I don't talk to Louie about it but he must know. At least when we pretend I'm not doing it, he has nothing to get mad about.

Love, Debra

September 25

Dear Mom,

I guess if it hadn't all happened in one day, I could have handled it better. First Louie came into the 2nd Chance when I was sitting at the bar. He asked me what I was doing there and I lied because I was turning tricks. I told him I was just there having a drink. Well, he'd known for weeks what I do at these bars on Wells St., but this time he pretended like he'd just figured it out. He went into a rage and started shrieking and hitting me until two men at the bar pulled him away and Burt the bartender told him he had to leave. But on the way out Louie said never to see him again.

I chased Louie out of the bar and followed him down Wells St. trying to explain, but he wouldn't listen. I told him that I had to make money somehow because he wasn't able to pay my way. He just got cruel then and said he never would pay the way of a common whore and if he wanted to get laid he certainly didn't need to buy some tramp to do it. That's

42

when I hit him and he knocked me down right in front of this cop at the corner of Wells and North Ave. I looked up at the cop and he was laughing. All he did was tell me to get up and get out of there.

And now I have this loose tooth, the little left fang beside my left molars, Mom. I just hope I don't lose it.

Anyway, I got up with blood dripping from my lip and from a cut in my mouth and ran off crying to the Farling Hotel to see Richard. I hadn't been back there in a few days. But when I arrived Jenns the manager was still at the desk, and he shoved all my bags with dresses and things piled in boxes out of the office, and he told me I'd been thrown out.

I asked him what for, and he said he was tired of the hookers in his hotel and was throwing us out. I asked if he'd keep my stuff until I found another room, because I knew I could always work out of the Lex down the street or even the notorious Mark Twain on Division if I had to. But I'm really scared of the Mark Twain, Mom, because of too many hookers and pimps. It's hard to stay independent when too many pimps are pressuring you. That whole scene just scares me.

So I asked if I could see Richard, and Jenns said no because Richard was still sleeping after getting off the night shift. I told him it was urgent, and Jenns just laughed and told me to get out.

Then I went into a rage, Mom. I can't tell you too much about it, but by the time the police arrived the lobby was all messed up with all the lamps broken and most of the chairs turned over, even the ones far too big for me to move, and Jenns was screaming like a madman.

So the cops came at me and I tried to hit one. But there were three of them and I had no chance. It was easy for them to handcuff my arms behind my back. But they weren't bad like some of the cops I'd dealt with. Of course, two of them already knew me from Wells St., but the third, the older one, was very nice. He asked me how old I was, and I lied, I told him I was 19, because I didn't want to be taken to Audy

Home for kids. He asked me if I'd gone to school in Chicago, so I made up a town in Missouri. He asked me all these nice questions and I lied about everything. But since I'd calmed down, he put the handcuffs on in front instead of in back, and that made me feel a lot better.

I bared my teeth at Jenns as they were taking me out the door, and the older cop told Jenns to keep my stuff until I got back for it. That must have made Jenns mad.

Anyway, Mom, they put me in the back of a paddywagon, and it's the first time I've ever been in one, and I found myself sitting opposite this big black woman. She wore this dirty black dress and had no shoes on her swollen feet. But she was singing this beautiful spiritual, Mom, and beating time with her toes. She had faith that no matter what was going to happen to her, Jesus would be there to take care of things. I somehow hoped that he'd have a little time left over to take care of me, but I knew that I couldn't sing for it the way she did, because she was so beautiful, Mom!

We drove quite awhile before they stopped and opened the back door to let us out. I asked the older cop where we were, and he told me Chicago State Mental Hospital. That made me feel good because it wasn't jail. The woman just kept singing all the while, and never did stop singing until they got us into a ward and a nurse shot her ass full of drugs to knock her out.

Anyway, the cops led us through the hospital to a big locked door. They knocked and the door was opened by somebody who obviously knew we were coming, a big angry nurse, almost as big as my gospel singer. They took us inside to the admitting desk and the cops talked to the angry nurse for awhile before taking our handcuffs off, and then right away they held the gospel singer and lifted up her skirt while a nurse shot her up. The black woman then staggered around singing off-key for a few more seconds before collapsing on the floor where everybody just left her. By everybody I mean the two nurses and two orderlies on duty.

The angry nurse then asked me some questions about myself. I lied on every one of them while she filled out the papers. The only truth I told was that my mother and father are dead. They didn't shoot anything into my ass though, I guess because they knew I was a little drunk and I told them I took drugs. So they didn't want to do anything to make me OD.

Not until they stopped questioning me and showed me my room and bed did I see that the place was filled with mad people of all types, all walking around like zombies. And if anyone would try to lie down on the floor or on a sofa, they would be hit and told to keep moving. I later found out that we weren't allowed to sleep during the day because then we wouldn't sleep at night, and the reason everybody was a zombie was because of the thorazine they shot into everybody's ass. The joint was a dancehall for us to do the thorazine shuffle.

It's when I saw this that I got scared, because I didn't want to be turned into a zombie, and I made a mistake. I said I was going to kill myself, in front of the nurses. Even the angry bitch nurse could hear me. The next thing I know is four men were hovering around me. They dragged me screaming into my room and pushed me down on my bed. I thought I was about to get raped, but what happened was worse. They strapped my arms and legs down.

When they left I lay on my back and stared up at the ceiling, but when I tried to move I discovered that I couldn't. I started to scream, I was in such terror. I don't know how long I screamed but finally a man who looked like he might be a doctor came in with a big pill he made me take. I thanked him because I knew the worst it could do was kill me and that was better than what I was going through.

I woke from this sleep when I felt something between my legs and opened my eyes to see this old madman with green snot running down his nose into his mouth, and he was fingering me. I shrieked at him to get out but he just smiled and continued to do it. So I just lay very still, Mom, and pretended to be dead. I couldn't really feel anything anyway. And then I felt I was standing over my body watching every-

45

thing, that I could see me dead and the madman playing with me. I could still feel his fingers in me and not even be there at the same time, except as an observer who didn't really care.

I don't know how long this went on, but a nurse finally did come in to tell the man to get out and leave me alone and to go wash his hands.

I think that's when I asked if I could get up to go to the bathroom. The nurse laughed a little bit and left. I guess she was telling me that I was already lying in my toilet, which turned out to be true, but by the time I peed all over myself and my bed I really didn't care anymore.

The madman with snot down his face came back in, but this time my screaming scared him off. Then a young nurse came in and asked me if I was all right. I immediately began to cry, Mom, because she was the first person in a long time who seemed to care. I asked her if she could help get me out of the restraints. She said she couldn't but she was my roommate and would help me all she could. She even got me a cup of water. And when she helped me drink it she sat at my side and stroked my hair and called me Nora.

I later learned that Nora was her daughter who died, and that had been the beginning of a long string of mental hospitals for her. She called a lot of us at Chicago State Nora, and I'm glad I was one of them, because she'd do anything for her Noras.

I can't tell you how long I lay there in my piss, but when they finally unstrapped me I couldn't move—my arms and legs were too stiff and weak—so I just lay there. Then at last I managed to work myself to the side of the bed and fall out, so there I lay flat on my stomach with something wet and stinky beneath my face. I was able to pull myself up enough to figure out it was a turd. I thought it might be mine but I wasn't sure. Just because I don't remember shitting in my bed doesn't mean that I didn't. Later I discovered that I hadn't shit in my bed, which means my face was on somebody else's crap.

Anyway, the shit beneath my face gave me added reason

to get up. Slowly my limbs began to work and I was able to push myself onto my hands and knees. I considered crawling out of my room but didn't want to do anything that might bother them, especially the big angry nurse, because I feared they'd just throw me back into restraints until I died.

Using my bed I finally pulled myself upright and was able to stand. I fell a few more times before I could walk. Then slowly I made my way out to the dancehall and the thorazine shuffle. You might think I was indignant with somebody else's shit on my face, but there was no dignity at Chicago State to worry about. Survival was the only concern.

Anyway, Mom, I made it to the bathroom to wash my face the best I could. I even took a pee in the toilet. But I was too constipated to go the other way.

When I got out of the bathroom a nurse screamed at me to clean up my bed and change my sheets. So I went back to my room and did the best I could wiping up my own piss with the piss-sopped sheet, because that's all I had to work with. Thank god for the plastic covering on the mattress. They threw a sheet in to me and I put it on my bed. Then I lay down to sleep but an orderly was in on me immediately to get up and join the others in the main room for the thorazine shuffle.

Every time I sat down in the main room to pretend to watch the television that was on all day, I'd start to nod out and somebody would scream and hit me. So I figured out that it was easier to keep walking with most of the others. We would all have our routes, it seemed. Mine was from the window to a chair, just back and forth like the zombie I was, with always too much drugs in me to come out of it. The hardest exercise I got all day was bending over for them to lift my smock and jam the needle in my butt. I bet I have more needle marks in my butt than most junkies ever get in their arm.

They'd bring in our tasteless meals and we'd all sit together in the dining room nodding over our plates. Few words were ever spoken, but more than one face would find

47

itself in its food until they'd scream and lift the head out of the plate and say something like what's the matter, Charlie, don't you like your food, or that's a good girl, Marjorie, just a few more bites. Like I said, there was no dignity left and we were all too drugged anyway.

I couldn't have told you how long I was there, maybe a few days, maybe a month, but Richard arrived. He told me that it had taken him a week to get me out of there.

Anyway, Richard got me signed out in his care somehow. They suggested to him that I seek out therapy and the possibility of a drug program. What a laugh that was. Anybody who ever goes to Chicago State needs a drug program before he gets out.

Richard took me back to the Farling Hotel and to his room where he was keeping all of my things. I was so happy to see my teddybear again. I might tell you why I never named it. It's because I knew it would leave me like all the others. So it was easier to just keep it as teddybear and not give it a name.

Anyway, I curled right up on Richard's bed with my teddybear and went to sleep, the first good sleep I'd gotten since being thrown into the madhouse. And when I woke Richard was there and he insisted that I take a shower, which I really wanted to do anyway because I still stank from pissing all over myself in Chicago State and not once could I take a shower there—or if I could, nobody told me about it and I was too drugged to care.

Anyway, Mom, when I woke up, that's when I had this real craving for some drugs, anything, because I was coming down from all that thorazine and crap at the hospital and I was really sick.

Richard had some pot and wine, thank god, and that was enough to get me fixed up and over to Wells St. to pick up a john.

Love, Debra

Dear Mom,

I know this will surprise you, but I'm in a small town called
Grinnell, IA. How did I get to Grinnell, IA? Well, I was
getting more and more depressed working the bars along
Wells St. and was drinking more and more.

Then I found myself drinking with this truck driver named
Stan, and we began to hop all around the bars, from Mother
Blues to the Earl to the Old Town Alehouse, and the next
thing I knew I was in this place balling Stanley. When we got
done, I still didn't know where we were, so I sat up and found
myself in the back of the cab of Stan's semi and we were in
this parking lot with a whole bunch of other trucks stopped
beside a freeway. Well, I still didn't know where I was until
Stan explained it—that we had closed O'Rourke's Pub where
all the writers and journalists drink and I had hitched onto
Stan's truck where he was delivering furniture to Des Moines
and Omaha.

I couldn't believe it, Mom, but we were in this truck stop
in Cedar Rapids, IA, and I was balling a truck driver in the
back of his cab.

Well, I was sick as a puppy and had to get out to vomit
beside Stan's truck. Then I was real hungry, so Stan took me
inside the restaurant for some breakfast. I went to the ladies
room and looked at myself, just like a tramp off Clark St.
who's about to die.

Then I looked in my purse to find it empty. I guess I'd
been robbed somewhere along the way. Well, it had happened
before. When I got back out to the booth with Stan, I told him
about it, and I could tell from his total disbelief that he
probably had at least some of it himself. Well, I didn't care.
At least he was man enough to buy the breakfast.

Being hung over and miles from home going to a place I
knew nothing about with a man I knew nothing about except
for his name, only made me more depressed when I thought
about it. Also, Mom, Iowa is not the prettiest state in the

union unless you like it flat and love cows. And this dumb hillbilly I'd taken up with was playing his cowboy music on the radio about as high as it can get. I think I even saw some cows run away when we passed. And after my time with Louie, if I never hear another country or folk song it will still be too soon.

I put up with this through half the state, it seems, and then I got excited because we came into Grinnell, and I know that you went to college at Grinnell before going to work in Milwaukee where you met Dad. So I asked this Stan to let me out and he pulled over the first place he could. I then did my little girl act and the bastard gave me $10 to survive on before shoving me out the door.

As I was walking off the highway I saw the sign to Chicago, only a few hundred miles, so I could always hitchhike back if things got too bad. Anyway I walked into this bit of a town and followed signs to this small Grinnell College. I recall how you told me that a railroad track went right through the center of campus. Well, Mom, that hasn't changed. It took no time at all to walk through the campus. There didn't seem to be much happening, just small groups of students and professors walking and pedaling bikes.

I found the student union and went in for a Coke and hamburger. And I sat down with some boy students who thought I was a coed, so I went to work to get a place for the night. I told them that I was hitchhiking through from Chicago on my way to San Francisco, which seemed as good an idea as the next.

So this nice-looking boy named Eddie took me to this restaurant and bar and we drank a few beers with his friends and later we went to a movie where we necked like kids, and then he took me back to his dorm to sneak me in and toss out his roommate (who pretended he had another place he had to sleep that night) and I gave Eddie the sweetest treatment I knew how. I don't think he'd had much experience with women before me, and by daybreak he was convinced of his undying love. I knew the last thing I could do was confess that I was only 15, which may have made me younger than his youngest sister and also would have made me "jail bait."

I could tell pretty quick that there really isn't anything to do in Grinnell, IA, and I'd go insane after awhile hiding out with my new young true love, so I got Eddie to take me to the Greyhound bus and buy me a ticket for Chicago. Of course, I told him I loved him and made up an address and telephone number where he could always reach me in Chicago. He gave me his telephone number and address in Grinnell, and I promised I'd be there for the homecoming dance and we both cried when he put me on the bus. (Yes, Mom, I cried and I meant it. Maybe it was because I just hated to leave anyone who really seemed to want me.)

As the bus pulled away for Chicago I waved to him and saw that he was still crying, and I was depressed all the way back to Chicago. I had learned to hate Chicago and the way I was living, but I didn't know what else to do. Maybe I should have continued on to San Francisco like I'd said.

Love, Debra

October 21

Dear Mom,

I had an abortion. It was either that or have a baby, and I wasn't about to have a kid. How would I take care of it? They'd only take it away from me anyway after they found out that I'm a 15 year old runaway hooker. Also the last thing I want is to put some poor creature into the world as it is today. What if it grew up like me?

So how it began is I started to get morning sickness. At first I thought I was just drinking too much. But I mentioned it at the Board of Health when I went there to get a VD check, and the doctor tested me, and sure enough I was pregnant.

Well, I've been pretty good about safe sex, like I told you, with the AIDS scare and all. But I haven't been perfect, like that time in the back of Stan's truck. The sonofabitch wasn't using anything, but what could I say?

Well, Mom, I know this girl on Well St., and she had a baby and the baby had AIDS. That's when they found out that she had AIDS too. They even found out that Robert has AIDS. That still doesn't keep Robert from running around Wells St. and fucking everything he can.

So I don't know what I've had contact with, and that includes the needles I used to share on occasion with people like Robert. And I'm not about to bear a kid with AIDS if I can help it.

I told Richard about it because he's the only person I trusted to help me, and he made an appointment for me at this abortion clinic on Michigan Ave. As the time for my abortion grew closer I got more depressed, just thinking I had my baby in me and was about to kill it, but that still made more sense to me than letting it live.

The morning arrived and Richard didn't bother to go to sleep after his shift. He took me out to breakfast and we talked about everything except what we were about to do.

But when Richard paid the bill and we walked out to catch a cab to our appointment, he said, "You know, you don't have to do this if you don't want to. We could raise it, you and I."

52

I laughed and told him he was a little too old to be the father of my kid, and he said he'd be the grandfather and the child would never know. But I told him that I really didn't want to raise a child in the Farling Hotel. He didn't argue about it any longer because I could tell he was too hurt by what we were doing.

Anyway, the cab arrived at the clinic for our 9:00 a.m. appointment, and we were greeted by a shouting snarling mob of right-to-lifers, and as we hurried past them into the clinic they yelled at us, calling me a whore and Richard a baby killer. I only looked at them once and I've never seen such hate. One man stood on the steps of the clinic carrying a big cross, but as he screamed at us, all I could see was that movie of Adolf Hitler howling at a rally as the crowd roared.

When we got inside and seated in the waiting room, I've never seen Richard so angry. Sometimes he'd moan and lash out as if killing someone. I'd try to joke him out of it but he'd just bounce back into his violent fantasy world. This, of course, meant that he wasn't there for me at that moment when I really needed him to hold my hand and comfort me. I don't think I've ever felt so wretched.

There were other girls waiting in the room with us, and I could tell they were scared and wretched too, listening to the mob outside.

At last I was called into a small room where the nurse harshly told me to get undressed and into a smock. Then I was made to lie back on an examining table with my legs spread.

I shut my eyes and tried to think this wasn't happening, and it really didn't take long. They sucked it out and it hurt a lot more than they said it would. Thank god, Mom, the nurse and doctor were nice, especially the nurse who held my face to her bosom when it was over and I was crying. She held me the same way I would have wanted you to do, Mom.

The right-to-life mob was even worse after Richard had paid the clinic and we left. They not only yelled at us, but they threw dirty diapers at us and condoms and teething rings.

Richard's head was just missed by a flying baby bottle. And while all this was happening, the Chicago police were there on their horses, but they just looked on and let it happen.

Thank god a courageous cabby pulled up and let us in. As we drove off showered by all sorts of things, the cabby called them a bunch of no good sonsofbitches. Then he told us he was studying for the ministry at Northwestern. That made me feel a little better, but still when we got back to the Farling all we could do was lie in bed with a bottle of wine. I cried, but we couldn't get ourselves to touch each other. We just drank until we passed out. And so much for child rearing, Mom.

That night, behind the desk, Richard really scared me for the first time, because he kept jumping up from the desk in a rage to bolt and stumble about the office in the fantasy of killing and maiming the people from that horrible mob.

That's when I knew I had to leave somehow. I had to get away from hateful Wells St. and Chicago before I got destroyed. But I watched Richard going through his violent fantasies and I wondered if it wasn't already too late.

Love, Debra

November 14

Dear Mom,
Richard has one night off, and that's Saturday. I guess we're both primarily night people because of our work, but there's little to do after the bars close at 4:00 a.m. except find an all-night restaurant or go home and read the Sunday paper early. It's probably Richard's hardest night. He seems to be much happier sitting behind the desk, because after he does the hotel books he just reads or talks to people all night.

I told you that Richard is in AA, but I've also told you how he's drunk with me on occasion, like the wine after my abortion. And once Richard gets started he sometimes doesn't stop for a few days. Still he's always made it to work and that's all the hotel cares about anyway. At the Farling, anything goes as long as you just show up.

So it was Saturday night and Richard and I were closing the Oxford Pub at 4:00 a.m., because that's where a lot of Richard's old drinking buddies hang out. Well, when it got beyond 3:00 a.m. I could tell that something was wrong with Richard. He was white and couldn't move, like a statue. I asked him what the matter was and he told me he was terri-fied, that he couldn't make it out the door. I saw him staring at a half-empty bottle of beer that somebody had left on the table before him. So what I did was take all the beer and booze glasses off the table and over to the bar to be washed. That relieved Richard a little, but still he couldn't get out of his chair. All this got a little boring until the joint finally closed and Richard was forced to leave.

He became animated when we were outside and suggested we walk through Lincoln Park to the lake. I told him the park is dangerous at night, with all the weirdos roaming, but Richard just lowered his voice and said don't worry about that, baby, with old Richard around.

So off we walked to the park, and believe me, Mom, I was really scared going through the viaduct under Lake Shore Drive to the beach, especially with Richard playing ghost

55

going OOOOOOOOOOO and AAAAAAAAA just to scare me more.

We got to the beach and listened to the water washing up and down the sand, and at that hour not even Lake Shore Drive was noisy. We seemed to have the place to ourselves. Richard didn't talk, but he put his arm around me and it made me feel very warm and good.

We walked far out on the breakwater, with the stars and half-moon shining over us, and I felt very small and protected somehow, like not just Richard but all this was holding me. Then Richard talked for the first time, whispering, "You know what all this is saying?"

I said no.

And he said, "It's telling us we're children of God and everything is all right."

I knew exactly what he was saying, and I bent back to kiss him through his red beard.

And he continued, "It's telling us that all our worries back there—" and he pointed toward the city "are bullshit, and it's all here, and it's all ours, and it's all right."

And I thought about that and how I'd turned three tricks that day, but not to worry because that didn't mean anything, and, Mom, I knew Richard was right.

And then, Mom, something horrible happened. We heard this man screaming on the beach. It was something in Spanish, so we couldn't tell what the matter was. But then almost immediately there appeared a police boat in the water with policemen looking over the side for something. And a fire truck pulled up to the beach. And several frogmen went into the water looking for something. Richard knew they were looking for some person. He said that someone had apparently drowned swimming at night, probably drunk, with his friend that was screaming. What they were doing swimming in November, I don't know! Then a helicopter came to skim the water along the beach. This went on for half an hour but nobody gave up. Until the frogmen found him and we saw the two frogmen racing out of the water, each pulling the arm of a man who was submerged beneath the water.

Right away they rolled him over and went to work on him, hitting his chest and giving mouth to mouth resuscitation, and the rescue truck drove right onto the beach to bring the oxygen for him. Then they loaded him into the truck and roared away with sirens screaming and a police car trailing.

Richard said that we were observing man at his best, but he said it was far too late because the man had been in the water too long before they found him. Too much brain deterioration, Richard said.

The next morning working the desk, Richard heard of the miracle, because the man had been taken to the hospital and was saved after all. I tingled all over when Richard told me, and I knew that the same policeman who could sit on a horse and do nothing when the mob at the abortion clinic was spitting and throwing things at us could work like this to save a man.

I also knew the man they saved, a Mexican or Puerto Rican probably, would not have been invited home to dinner by the Irishmen who pulled him from the lake, and if he tried to move into some of their Irish neighborhoods he might get stoned to death.

But it was good to see man at his best instead of his worst. Then I got very sad, Mom, thinking that I only knew man at his worst doing what I do, and Richard and I talked about this. Then he said a kid should never have to do what I do. This meant he cared, and I loved him very much. The only time I loved him more, I guess, was when he gave me my teddybear, and someday I'm going to name that teddybear because I'm beginning to think it won't run away after all. Maybe Richard won't run away either.

Then I asked him, "Richard, do you think we'll ever get out of the Farling Hotel? Do you think we'll ever get away from Wells Street?"

And he said, "People die to get away from here."

I didn't laugh.

Then he said, "What about California? Have you ever thought about going to California?"

And I said, "What for? To dig for gold?"

He laughed, then got very serious to say, "Maybe."

Love, Debra

November 17

Dear Mom,

Last night I got in from Wells St. to see that Richard was all beat up behind the desk. His face was all misshapen with two black eyes and his left arm obviously hurt when he moved it. I asked him what had happened and he told me that big Rolph had come in drunk and had molested him behind the desk.

I asked what he'd done to let Rolph behind the desk in the first place, and Richard said he hadn't expected trouble from Rolph or he would have had the door locked. I told him that I'd always known Rolph to be an asshole because every time I saw him he made a pass at me.

It turns out that Richard and Rolph had an argument and Rolph had come behind the desk and yanked off half of Richard's beard. When Richard put a hand on him, Rolph dislocated Richard's left shoulder merely by hitting his arm. Then Rolph had finished him off with a few punches to the head.

"Well," I said, "did you get the police?"

Richard went into one of his violent paroxysms, beating up the phantom before him, so I waited for him to finish before asking again if they'd gotten the police.

"You know better," said Richard. "Jenns and Rolph are old buddies, you know that. They get drunk together in each other's room."

I could tell that Richard was in some kind of shock. "Look, Richard," I said. "I think we'd better get out of here. It's too rough and dangerous."

Richard didn't say anything and I sat with him for a long time. I was waiting for Rolph to come back because I had my mace. I've gotten to know something about Richard. He doesn't defend himself very well. He's too sensitive, and when he gets mad he either takes it out on his fantasies or on himself. Some day I suspect Richard might just flip out altogether. Then he'll either kill everything in sight or put a bullet in his own brain. He told me a long time ago that the reason he'd never have a weapon around is fear that he'd use it.

Richard went through his violent fantasy act repeatedly while I watched him. He'd flail the air and make animal noises. I also worried that he might be hurt with a concussion maybe. But mostly I just waited for Rolph with my mace.

Then Richard got a call on the switchboard and I could tell it was Rolph. After awhile, Richard was laughing and saying that's okay, it's just one of those things, and I knew Rolph was apologizing. When the conversation was over I asked Richard what it was about and he just said Rolph's all right now and had asked if Richard knew how he could get a woman to spend the night.

"Still drunk?" I asked.

"Very," Richard said, massaging his left shoulder.

"Well, why don't you call him back? Tell him you're sending him a hooker."

Richard looked at me quizzically, then got angry. "If you ever touch Rolph, I'll never see you again. I'll see to it that you're thrown out of here and can never get back in!"

I walked to Richard and kissed his swollen face. Then I took out my can of mace and held it in front of him. "Don't worry about me," I said. "I just want to thank him for this beautiful night."

Richard stood up and howled, "No, it's gone far enough! He's apologized, and it's over!"

"Until the next time he drinks."

"The next time he drinks I'll have the office door locked."

59

"That's no way to have to live, Richard. What's his room number?"

"Look," Richard said, "I won't have you getting hurt just to take revenge for me."

But I was already looking down at the books and I'd found Rolph's room number.

"I won't have you going up there," Richard insisted. "He's probably asleep by now anyway. It's over, let's forget about it."

"We have to get out of this hotel!"

"Yes, that's probably a good idea."

"And out of Chicago."

"We'll talk about it."

I told Richard I was tired and if he didn't mind, I'd go to his room to bed now. I could tell he was still frightened from all that had happened to him, but of course he let me go and said he'd be up later.

But I didn't go to Richard's room. I went to Rolph's door on the third floor on the other side of the hotel. I stood in front of it for a long time and I could hear him moving about and singing, even laughing a little bit. It took me awhile to get up the nerve, but then I knocked.

"What do you want?" he growled through the door.

"The desk clerk said you wanted a woman," I said, with my hand on the mace in my pocket.

He opened the door and stared down at me through one eye so as not to see double, he was so drunk. "Ah ha," he muttered, "so Richard is lending me his bitch. I should kick the shit out of him more often."

I smiled and slid past him, then waited for him to shut the door and turn toward me before I let him have it full in the face. He fell helplessly, like a tree with muscular dystrophy. I sat on the bed until his hulk started to get it back together, then I maced him again. I planned to do this all night. This Rolph was every man who's ever touched me. He was my father coming drunkenly into my room at night while I'd hear you, Mom, crying in your bedroom. I knew this could kill him, but I didn't care—until I looked at a bottle beside his bed on the table. I picked it up and looked at it—nitroglycerine for the heart. Rolph the giant had a heart problem. I looked down at him, and he wasn't writhing. Instead he lay still. I bent close enough to see that he was breathing, but even if he was I knew I'd be in trouble for this.

So I hurried down to the desk and told Richard what I'd just done.

He thought for a moment and said, "Well, you're right. Even if you didn't kill him, we can't stay here." He started for the door. "I think the desk can take care of itself until morning." Out of the money drawer he took what the hotel owed him for work that week and we were off.

It only took us an hour to get all our stuff piled into the back of Richard's old Ford. We left most of his books. Good riddance, he said, it would be nice to be free of them, and off we headed toward California.

I hoped we'd pass Grinnell again, Mom, to see the place you went to college one last time. And that's exactly what we did. We didn't stop though. I didn't want to. I really didn't want to take even the small chance of seeing Eddie.

Love, Debra

December 21

Dear Mom,

Chicago had had a beautiful fall, and all the trees were so colorful in Lincoln Park that we could sit there and forget our troubles for awhile. But I'm glad we escaped Chicago before real winter arrived.

Richard and I had no idea how fortunate we were to leave when we did, because finally, after 3 days of incessant driving, trying to sleep in the car to save money, we arrived in San Francisco to these great hills and water all around us with the ocean and the bay, and I read a Chronicle to discover that Chicago was just beginning another winter of misery, with its first snowstorm and zero degree weather. San Francisco, Mom, is always mild and magnificent.

Of course, after a week of living in a hotel off the Tenderloin, we both had to go to Welfare to get General Assistance. Richard got on it okay, but I didn't have the papers. For one thing, I needed a birth certificate to prove I'm an adult, and I'm still faking it, even if I have become 16 now. I spent my sweet 16 birthday crammed into an old Ford en route to California.

But we were lucky in a way, Mom, because we never had to live in the streets of San Francisco. We did eat our meals at St. Anthony's and Martin de Porres' free dining rooms, and Richard got a single room at the Gates Hotel off the Tenderloin and I was able to sneak in every night. If we'd had to pay for a double we couldn't have made it.

Richard made the rounds of the hotels and was surprised to discover that he couldn't just become an immediate desk clerk in San Francisco. There are too many people here trying to squeak by, and jobs like desk clerk are always hard to get. If he hadn't sold his car to some low roller on Mission for $200 we never could have made it.

Anyway, Mom, Richard and I walked up from the Tenderloin, which is a lot like Clark St. or Wilson Ave. in Chicago where the flops and strip joints and the hookers are, through

62

Haight St. to Golden Gate Park. And Golden Gate Park is the most beautiful city park you can imagine. It has different kinds of trees from what you find in Chicago and different plants and flowers too. It has these amazing bottle-brushes on its bushes, which are red flowers that actually look like bottle-brushes—honest, Mom, they do.

Well, we walked through some playgrounds and some woods and found ourselves at the Academy of Sciences, a little museum that would make you laugh it's so small compared to the Museum of Science and Industry or the Field Museum in Chicago. Like at the Field Museum, Mom, there are a million dinosaurs, but at this little Academy of Sciences there's just this one little bitty dinosaur. But Richard had this idea that he might just as well see if the Academy needed a guard. And the first person he met was a tall guard named Jack Reilly, who took him to the head guard, a big black man named Duke, and sure enough Richard became a part-time guard at the Academy.

He hates it, of course, because it's a lot more work than sitting behind a hotel desk all night reading books, but he's able to play guard with his big red beard while reading on duty. Duke doesn't like his reading on duty, but he does it anyway. Reilly doesn't mind, because Richard still does his job, and Richard likes the other guards because he says they're as crazy as himself.

Part-time at the Academy means 6 or 7 days a week, and Richard got pretty surly the first couple of weeks. On several occasions he lost his temper and mouthed off at Duke at the wrong time and place, and he won't shave his beard like Duke keeps asking him to, so we never know for sure when Richard will get canned, but he hasn't yet.

It wasn't as easy for me to get a job. I knew I could always hook in the Tenderloin, but just the suggestion angered Richard who says we are in San Francisco now and this is a new life. But after awhile I did get a job, washing dishes and cleaning up in a bakery. It's only 4 hrs. a day, but it's paid under the table so no taxes are taken out, and combined with Richard's paycheck we can get by.

We moved out of the Tenderloin to a studio apartment in the Inner Sunset a few blocks from the park and the museum. That way Richard can walk to work. I can too if I want, but the bakery is a little farther away.

Anyway, our studio is so much bigger than anything Richard and I have lived in before. Most people could not live long in even a big one-room apartment like ours, but to us this is luxury and we have a big kitchen too. And our window faces west toward the beach and we can look out at Golden Gate Park and even see part of the bridge. And, Mom, I've never seen such skies. People here complain about the fog because that's all they have to complain about. They've never lived through Chicago summers and winters. But I love our fog. It seldom stays all day, and the sky is changing all the time in the most splendid colors, especially as the sun sets over the ocean and the bay.

Richard and I like to walk through the park all the time. We walk past a field of buffalo—really, Mom, buffalo—right here in the city, and end up at Ocean Beach. Lake Michigan is nice, but it's so small and trivial in comparison, with those giant salt waves here climbing so high and beating up onto the sand. And it's so clean, with so few people, and you can walk for miles on it. You can walk up a hill to the Cliff House and look down at Seal Rock where all the seals honk away, and there are a million sea birds with them. Then you walk on past the remains of the old Sutro bathhouse and find yourself on cliffs looking down over the entrance to San Francisco Bay. And then the sun comes down over the bay and the hills of Marin. And, Mom, I'd tell you all this is beautiful but I can't tell it for what it is, I can't do it justice.

I only wish you'd lived long enough to have seen some of this yourself.

We live in a small neighborhood filled with little shops and bookstores and cafes. I go sit in a cafe called the Owl and

Monkey and I sip my coffee and just think, wow, Mom, I'm here in San Francisco, I'm here!

Love, Debra

January 7

Dear Mom,

Working at the bakery is kind of fun. I know you must find this a surprise because as I told you, I'm the dishwasher and cleanup person and you know how much I hated to do that at home. I hate to do it at my apartment with Richard too, and I must confess that I've done everything to manipulate Richard into doing most of the work—like I have never washed the floors and never take out the garbage. I know if I just wait long enough Richard will swear and snarl and do all that. Neither one of us care to make the bed, so it's never made. I am willing to do the wash half the time though, but that's because I hate the way Richard never folds the clothes and mine come out all wrinkled.

Still, working at the bakery is different, because every Friday Jake the owner pays me my $100 (or more if I work overtime) and it's all like a big game there, with only Jake taking anything very seriously. Along with Jake doing the books and getting the business, there's his two bakers, skinny hatchet-faced Hannah who just passed the bar examination but can't get the job she wants in law, and the fat dike Jenny who is drunk all the time and robs Jake blind whenever she has the chance. Sometimes she passes out drunk at the bakery and Jake has to drive her home. Why he doesn't fire Jenny nobody knows, but it seems the more incompetent you are, the more Jake feels he has to take care of you. (Maybe that's why he likes me, because I'm too short to lift the big pots to hang them on their hooks.) Then there's tall college boy type Michael who goes out to sell our wares to stores and restaurants, and stocky Peter.

65

Peter is the delivery man, driving the cakes and tarts all over the city in his beat-up Volkswagen, and he's more like a young frisky ape than anything else. He's 19 years old and runs around the bakery jumping up on things and making funny weird noises and, Mom, he's as funny as anything I ever see on television. I sometimes wonder if Richard wasn't like this when he was younger. Of course I could never picture Peter reading a book. He isn't as smart as Richard. Peter thinks he's some kind of punk in his leather jacket and purple hair with one big earring like a big gold moon hanging from his left ear.

Anyway, Mom, right away I knew Peter liked me because he'd do things like jump on the dough I had rolled out on the table and pick me up to seat me in the bowl of chocolate. And the more Jake would yell at him, the weirder Peter would become. One afternoon when I came in to clean up the place, I opened the back door to find Peter hanging upside down with his legs hooked over a pipe that runs along the ceiling. His tongue was out and his hands hung down like he was dead and he didn't move until I screamed. (I didn't really think he was dead, Mom, I was just playing with him.)

Then he dropped, doing a somersault to land on his feet, and told me he'd been waiting for the past hour that way for me to come in so he could scare me. Boy, did I laugh. And Peter jumped around me saying chee chee like a monkey and scratching under his arms until he grabbed me. I expected him to put me in the bowl of chocolate again or maybe lift me up on a shelf with the boxes, but instead he kissed me. And since we were the only ones there he held the kiss a long time.

None of this surprised me, Mom. I knew Peter was shy and this is the only way he could get around to kissing me.

Well, he didn't have to stay when I was cleaning the place, but he did anyway, and he even bought a pizza for us down at the corner. I wasn't hungry but I ate it, just to please him, and he wanted to buy me some ice cream too, but I said no because I knew I'd explode.

Anyway, while I cleaned up and washed the pots and

silverware, Peter told me about himself. You know, Mom, he was a third-string All-State center on his high school football team, chosen by the Omaha Herald when he was a senior, and he had a football scholarship to the University of Nebraska and played his freshman year before he banged up his knee. So he dropped out of college and came to San Francisco, the biggest city he's lived in outside of Lincoln, Nebraska, because he was raised on a farm.

I guess that's how he got so strong, all that farm work and football.

When he drove me home he kissed me goodnight and gave me a chocolate cake. I don't think Jake would have liked that but I wasn't going to refuse anything Peter gave me, because I really liked him, Mom.

Richard was home reading as usual. He wanted a piece of the cake but I told him he couldn't have any until I had a piece too, but just then I was too full. I guess that wasn't very nice to Richard, but I just didn't feel right letting him have the first piece of cake Peter gave me.

When Richard asked why I was so late, I lied that I'd gone out for pizza with the staff at the bakery, and he said that I might have called him, because he hadn't eaten yet. This made me feel bad because of course Richard and I always had dinner together. So I made him some eggs and then I cut him a big piece of the cake. I sat with him as he ate dinner and even wanted to do his dishes—but I really couldn't go that far.

Later when we got into bed I knew he sensed something was wrong from the way he pressed up against me. We are pretty affectionate, Mom, but we don't have a sexual relationship, even sleeping together. There was nothing wrong with him pressing against me, though, and I knew he didn't want more, but this time all my rage came out. I don't know what it is, but sometimes I hate all men so much I just want to kill them, and I take it out on Richard because he's around me all the time.

Anyway, Mom, I hit him and pushed him away and told

him to keep his hands off me. He didn't say anything. He just rolled over with his back toward me. I couldn't sleep because it made me feel so bad.

And I knew I couldn't tell him about Peter.

Love, Debra

January 26

Dear Mom,

Peter started staying late with me at the bakery, which made it take longer to do my work because we started balling on the sofa. We'd wait until nobody was there but us, and we'd ball. It got to where I couldn't think of anything else but going to work and balling Peter.

I think Jake knew what was going on and he commented to us both that our work had slipped a bit, but he only said it once. Anyway, we kept doing it. It was easier than talking. If I had anything to talk about, I usually did it with Richard because he was still my best friend, but I couldn't tell him what I was doing with Peter.

I wondered why Peter never offered to take me out, even for a cup of coffee away from the bakery, and we never contacted each other over the weekend. Of course I knew I was trying to keep everything from Richard. But sometimes Peter and I would lie on the couch and discuss living together, even getting married and having children. I guess I really loved Peter, Mom, but then he told me he was living with some other woman and had been for over a year.

This was like getting stomped on the stomach. I cried and told him he didn't love me, but he said he did and took me to the couch to ball away my tears. Then he told me he never really loved this Carol he was living with, but he needed a place to stay when he arrived from Nebraska and after meeting Carol in a bar on Haight St. she asked him to move in with her until he'd got it together. She had a 2 year old kid, but Carol never really knew who the father was. Well, Peter started sleeping with Carol and really liking the baby, so he stayed.

I asked him to move out and live with me if he loved me. But he said he just couldn't do that because he owed Carol too much after all she'd done for him.

Then Peter started to lose interest in me, almost like he never should have told me, and we began to ball less and less on the couch. We still did it sometimes, but it was almost like some of the johns I used to date, when nobody much cares. He also got more and more somber and he stopped joking around, until everybody in the bakery felt it. He never told anyone what was going on, not even me, but I knew it involved what was going on with me and him and Carol.

I guess I wasn't putting on a very good show for Richard either, because he kept asking me what's wrong. I kept telling him nothing, but I think I was the most unhappy girl in San Francisco while this was going on.

Then one day at work Peter was really low, almost like he couldn't even move. Jake, who's a big-armed, powerful-looking man himself, even got mad at Peter's moping and pushed him, but Peter just kept moping. At the end of the day, when everybody was gone but us, Peter just sat in a chair and stared at me cleaning up. I really didn't want anything more to do with him at the moment, so not one word was exchanged.

Until at last he said, "Carol asked me to leave."

I felt this real joy rise in me and I asked him what he planned to do.

"I don't know," he said.

"What do you mean, you don't know," I said. "This is our chance. We'll get a place together. You'll move out from Carol and I'll move out from Richard." Even when I said this I felt a rush of terror, because I liked living with Richard. I was afraid of moving away from him.

"It's not all that easy," he grumbled.

Then I got mad. It was one thing for me to be scared about moving away from Richard, but I hated to think that Peter might be scared about moving from his Carol. "What do you mean, it's not that easy!" I screamed. "You've got to move out anyway, so let's just do it!"

Then he did something that really surprised me. He jumped up from his chair and hit me. I don't think I've ever been hit so hard, because the first I recalled I was sitting on the floor shaking my head.

And he yelled down at me, "I don't want any slut to tell me what to do, you or anyone else, you hear?"

Since I was really afraid of him then, I nodded my head yes and he ran out of the bakery.

I was able to work a little longer, but I was all alone and that neighborhood in the Western Addition wasn't the best anyway. Any crazy man could have just walked in to hurt me. But what I was really afraid of was Peter, that he'd come back and hit me again. So I left the place dirty with dishes piled up everywhere. I'd walked several blocks before recalling that I hadn't locked up, but I was too scared to go back.

I got back to the apartment just when Richard was leaving to sit in the Owl and Monkey with his book. I could tell from looking at him that he knew someone had beaten me up, and I've never seen him angrier. So I told him what had happened.

"Why did Peter do this?" he asked.

"Because he's crazy," I said. "His girlfriend has just thrown him out and he flipped."

He started to walk away and I asked him where he was going, and he said to find Peter. I grabbed him, because I knew that my 50 year old hero would get the worst of an insane Peter and then Peter would make it worse yet by telling Richard he'd been balling me all this time.

As Richard pushed me away he asked me where Peter lived, and thank god I didn't know. So Richard just took me back into our apartment and looked at my swollen head, just like his that night at the Farling Hotel, he said. Then he said that life can be very horrible and sad. And with this we both lay on the mattress to hold each other and cry.

I'm glad I never told Richard about Peter and me being in love. After thinking about it I guess we never were. Maybe it was just something to do for awhile, to pick life up a bit and make the waters move. Well, it did that all right.

Richard forbade me to return to that bakery job, but I told him this could never happen again. It only happened because Peter had been thrown out by his girlfriend. And not to worry about me, because I could handle it. I didn't want to admit to myself that part of me still loved Peter, and I wanted to find out if things could get patched up again somehow.

Anyway, the next day with my head aching I returned to work. I told Jake what had happened and Jake just stomped around the bakery waiting for Peter to come in because he was going to fire him and maybe even get him arrested. This, of course, is not what I wanted, but I didn't have to worry about it because Peter never did come in that day. And he didn't come in the next either.

But the day after that a policeman came in and talked to Jake. And when he left Jake came to me and put his arm around me because he knew that something had been going on with Peter and me, and that's when Jake told me that Peter had been fished out of the bay. He had jumped off the bridge.

I don't know what it is about me, Mom, but everything I touch seems to turn to shit. I never told you this, but I know the reason you drank yourself to death is because I'm a bad girl. And I always felt that Daddy used to come into my bedroom to play with me at night because I'm bad. Because why is it that all these things happen when I'm around?

And I get scared about Richard too. He's the only person to treat me like I'm a little decent, so I'm afraid of what I'll do to him. Like, Mom, what if I'd told him about Peter and me? Maybe Richard would have hit me as hard as Peter did.

And then maybe Richard would have jumped off the bridge.
You know, Mom, maybe I should jump off the bridge. It
might be the best thing for everybody.

Love, Debra

Dear Mom,
I couldn't really do my work at the bakery anymore, not after
Peter jumped off the bridge. Sometimes I couldn't even show
up, and if I did I was never on time. Jake would plead with
me. He said he understood I missed Peter but still he had a
business and the Board of Health would condemn him if I
didn't do my job. I told him I was doing my best, but I wasn't
even trying. That made the bakers mad too, because then they
had to wash out their own pots if they were to get anything
done.

So I lasted one more week at the bakery and Jake said he'd
risk another week if I was willing to see a shrink. I told him
where he could shove his shrink and he told me to get lost.

Richard was as supportive as he knew how to be, especially since he didn't really know why I'd be that upset over
Peter jumping off the bridge. He told me I could relax until I
felt better and he wasn't going to force me to work. That was
all very nice of him, but after he paid the rent all by himself
we had exactly no money for food or anything else.

Then we had a real argument because I decided to try
prostitution again. Richard said no way, even after I told him
I wouldn't work the Tenderloin, that I'd work Fisherman's
Wharf instead where my clients would be more middle class
and safe.

So, completely frustrated I screamed, "Okay, Richard,
then what do you think we should do?"

"Don't worry about it," he said. "Things like this tend to
take care of themselves."

Then I got mad, because it wasn't all me. Richard has gotten himself down to working no more than 2 or 3 times a week. When the museum calls him to work more, he just says he doesn't want to. So there we were, a part-time museum guard who didn't want to work and an unemployed girl, with no way to make ends meet. Peter's way began to seem like a good idea.

But Richard finally said something constructive. Why not both of us go over to the Division of Vocational Rehabilitation and find out what we can do? So we called Voc Rehab and set up appointments. And when Richard would be working as a guard I'd sneak on over to Fisherman's Wharf and turn a few tricks, but I could never tell Richard about this. Still it was the only way we could have paid the bills that month.

I got the right IDs made for me in this little shop on Market Street. They all say I am 21 years old. At 16 I have no trouble passing for that.

Anyway, I told the Voc Rehab counselor that I'd been a waitress in Chicago before coming to San Francisco and that's all I knew how to do, but at this point I didn't really want to be a waitress anymore. So they gave me some tests and decided I should be working with people, and they had just the right position for me. I would be a rehab worker with alcoholics. This made me laugh, Mom, because you died of drinking and Daddy I'm almost sure was an alcoholic, and there I was set up to work with them.

So they sent me to the Ozanam Center, a big barn of a place on Howard St. where all the winos and street derelicts end up. Of course most of them just hang around and die, but a few get started off to recovery.

At first I thought the job was kind of easy—making coffee for the drunks, cleaning up, changing beds, signing them in and trying to talk them into drying out and going to rehab programs. But the job is beginning to wear on me. I see too many drunks who never can get it together. They seem to like me because they think I am young and pretty. The staff likes me too—from the director to the counselors down to the workers on my level. We aren't paid much more than minimum wage, but it's looked at as training to go onto better things in the alcoholism field. And most of the workers are recovering drunks and addicts just getting it back together themselves, and they can look at this job as a step up from where they've been.

The place is packed all day with shrieking alkies, either attempting to get sober or just getting in for a cup of coffee and some talk. Those seeking programs to get well are allowed upstairs where they can sleep and be fed until we can get them off to the Salvation Army 28-day program or maybe AETC treatment program at San Francisco General Hospital, and some of the lucky ones we send to a longer, more extensive program at Redwood City.

Of those we send to programs, only a few ever make it to sobriety for any length of time. Most of them end up coming back to go through the whole painful process again. That probably hurts the most, seeing the center used as a revolving door.

But something else bothers me too. The staff often seem as crazy or crazier than the men we treat. It isn't unusual to see a staff member go back to drinking himself and return to the gang of clients at the center.

This type of sick rotation of bodies has become a way of life for so many of the Ozanam crowd, Mom, that I know I have to detach from everything that's going on around me if I am to work this job and survive.

Unfortunately, a faction of the staff handles the situation by doing their own drugs. They pop Valium or whatever else they need to function, and since many of them are druggies and alkies themselves, usually in initial stages of recovery, this soon gets them back into practicing their addictions. And of course this is all terrible for morale, especially since some of these chippies are full-time counselors and even supervisors. And the head honcho, an ex-offender named Brandt, has to know about all this since he himself went up through the

74

ranks at Oz, but he acts blind and deaf about it all, probably realizing that he can never keep a totally clean and sober staff at a jungle like this, so it's better to be blind and deaf than short-handed.

So, Mom, you see the type of situation I'm working in. It can really get a little depressing. But I'm happy that there are a few friends I work with, like this older woman Harriet. She's been in Alcoholics Anonymous for 30 years and has been working in the alcoholism field now for over 20, and she's very nice. She treats me like her granddaughter.

But there's one thing about me, Mom, that has always gotten me into trouble. As soon as things get rough, I want somebody to be around to save me, which means by loving me to let me know I'm okay. Somebody like Harriet is good for this, but it usually turns out to be men. I think that's what I always liked about hooking. At the same time that doing it made me feel horrible, I'd feel good with men holding me and loving me. So I'd feel worthless and needed at the same time.

So what happens at Ozanam Center is we get these beat-up men, and some of them aren't very old, and after they get cleaned up and into some nice enough clothes they can look pretty nice, Mom, but they're really needy and love to flirt with me. Harriet is always warning me not to take any of them at all seriously, and of course the more she cautions me the more exciting it all becomes.

Then of course there's still Richard, and I never want to hurt Richard, but he comes on more and more like a father and I kind of resent that. So part of me wants to break away from him, and even though I'm guilty about what I did with Peter I'm also mad that Peter and I weren't strong enough to have pulled it off—like I resent that I'm not strong enough to break away from Richard. So when I see these good-looking men just off the streets who need me, Mom, I have to be careful.

Love, Debra

Dear Mom,

It's been ages since I've written to you, and I'm sorry. I guess Ozanam and Richard just kept me too busy.

Richard has found that the longer he guards at the museum the more he hates it. He says the hardest work he's ever done is standing around all day doing nothing. Of course part of Richard's problem is that he doesn't just do nothing. He waits until he thinks his supervisors aren't looking and then he pulls a book out of his back pocket to read, and the Academy of Sciences be damned! Naturally this has caused some friction and as much as Richard might complain, it's hard to blame the museum entirely for wanting him to do his job.

But then Richard did something exceedingly clever. He applied for unemployment insurance on the basis of the museum not giving him enough days to work. Of course the reason he isn't working enough days is because he refuses to work them when called. But still the State of California found Richard eligible for unemployment, and the museum was too dumb to dispute it. And to add to the absurdity, the museum still calls Richard in to work occasionally, even though he's screwed them for the unemployment, and Richard will accept one day a week because he can do that without destroying his unemployment claim which allows him to make up to $25 more than his weekly claim payment on any given week.

Do you understand any of this, Mom? What it comes down to is the State is paying Richard $82 a week, but he can also make $25 from another source which is the Academy.

This means that Richard has to make do on a maximum of $107 each week, which to most people would not be near enough but to Richard is Heaven because the most important thing is not having to work very much. And as long as I religiously bring home my pay from the Ozanam detox job, which even on my best week never comes to more than $150 clear, we can get by. (Of course, as long as I've been with Richard I've always brought home more money than he has.)

But Richard decided to upset the balance because he said he was tired of staying in San Francisco all the time. It was time to head down to Santa Barbara, to swim and live on the beach, and the devil with working even one day a week at the Academy of Sciences, because Richard needed a rest.

So off we hitched down Hwy 1 to see the coast and Big Sur on down to Santa Barbara. Our first ride was from a young pig farmer, and Richard and I had to ride in the back of the pickup truck where the pigs usually rode. We carefully set our bags and bodies in there not to be plopped in pigshit, but still by the time we were let off on the other side of Monterey we both stunk of pig.

The old woman who picked us up and took us the rest of the way had a nose too old to smell anything I guess, because she never complained. She never stopped talking either, and I'm just glad Richard was in the front to pretend interest as she howled about how nice we were, this dear family of father and daughter who hitchhiked together. "Most of the younguns won't let the old ones hitchhike with them," she said, as if she knew a lot about it. Richard just kept nodding his head all the way to Santa Barbara.

When she let us out of her old Buick we checked a few hotels to discover that even the slummiest were too expensive for us. But Richard said that maybe that was good because now we'd save money by sleeping on the beach.

So after an afternoon of swimming in some of the biggest breakers in history and walking all around pretty Santa Barbara which was preparing for its big annual sports festival next week, we ate at a cheap Mexican restaurant and by the time the sun went down we were all ready for sleep.

But, Mom, this wasn't liberal San Francisco. This was fascist country where Ronnie Reagan and his gang of bandits have their ranches. I was awakened by something hitting my head and I sat up to find a cop above me tapping my skull with a nightstick. I just stood up, but Richard was not so docile. He jumped up calling them a bunch of blue-balled

77

bastards. He stopped shouting though after they worked him over a little.

The police hauled a few more people in off the beach, and in the paddywagon this streetperson said that things had changed in Santa Barbara. They used to try to take care of their people. Now all they did was put you in jail and drive you outside the city to drop you off. This was especially so come festival time when the merchants wanted the streets free for tourists.

Anyway, I spent the night with a handful of drunken hookers and women derelicts, while Richard spent the night in the men's tank. There was no way to sleep with so many drunks moaning and screaming. And the next morning we didn't even go before the judge. We just got shoved back into the paddywagon and driven out beyond Summerland.

I was sure the cops must have taken our money that Richard was carrying, but all they did was get the $5 out of his pocket. They never found the $40 he had in his sock. So we walked into Summerland to swim and lie on the beach most of the day. Then starving, we went into town to have an omelet.

After that, it was already evening and we started hitching back to San Francisco, but it wasn't as easy this time. It was almost dark before a college kid picked us up on his way to Cal-Poly. He was probably regretting it when he smelled us with our pigshit and night in jail, but he took us all the way to San Luis Obispo where we sat in a Swenson's Ice Cream until we were too exhausted, then we walked out until we found a schoolyard to curl up together in a doorway away from the street.

I don't recall a thing until the birds woke us in the morning. I was cold, so we found a deli in town where we washed up and had a good breakfast.

Then we got lucky, because we immediately got picked up by a mad speed freak at the edge of town and he had us back to San Francisco in no time.

By then Richard and I were too wasted to speak. We just showered and went to bed. And so much for our first vacation away from the city.

Love, Debra

Dear Mom,
Back in mid June the Academy decided it had had enough of Richard. No longer would they call him into work, and that means his income has dropped to the mere $82/week the State is sending him for unemployment, and I'm concerned because a couple times I've come home from Oz and smelled wine on his breath. You can't work at a detox without being concerned about this sort of thing, especially with Richard's record of having to get on Alcoholics Anonymous in Chicago. And then, of course, after going to a couple San Francisco meetings Richard has decided he can handle the problem on his own.

Also, Richard is getting crazier. He worries more and more about his economic condition and obsesses about ways to get by without working because he can't get himself to look for a job.

They put out a sign for kitchen help at the Owl and Monkey but Richard wouldn't ask for the job. They also had a sign for a dishwasher at the Raintree where we have breakfast now and then, but Richard wouldn't apply there either. It seems the more he obsesses and worries the less he can do anything about it, and his unemployment is running out.

At last Richard has come up with his most enterprising scheme—Welfare. He'll get back on General Assistance. He knows that he'll have to apply as an alcoholic because that way they have him get a form signed every day saying he's been to an AA meeting. This will get him back committed to

AA, which I appreciate, but his reason is to keep from sweeping the streets 3 mornings a week, which the non-alkies on GA have to do.

All this is okay with me because it will keep Richard from drinking anymore and assure him enough income to pay his share of the bills.

But of course I'm beginning to resent Richard. Our relationship has gone from his being my daddy in Chicago to my being his mommy in San Francisco. And the more helpless Richard becomes the more I resent him. But I don't know what to do about it because I still feel I need him, and that of course makes me even madder.

I have no way to show my anger because I still feel like I owe Richard a lot for all he's done for me and he isn't doing anything overt to hurt me. He's just changing, I might even say getting worse somehow, but how can I get mad at him for that?

So, Mom, I express my anger the way I've always expressed it when I have no other way. I found a man—this quiet, dignified, professorial alkie who has just detoxed at Oz and is working and living on the second floor until they have an opening for him at Redwood City. We talk in the lounge and he of course plays father and I go into my little girl's role. We exchange our mutual feelings of love in the laundry room downstairs where he kisses me.

After a while I could tell from observing him that my middle aged darling had turned into a 14 year old puppy of joy. So I found one of the young workers downstairs who only lives a few blocks away and after flirting with him several hours where my old puppy could see it, I went with the young man to his apartment one afternoon and got laid. Actually it was kind of nice, because I'd been good for a long time. When I got back late to work, my sweet puppy asked me where I'd been and of course I told him.

Then I felt horrible, Mom, because the old fool walked out of detox and before the week was out the MAP truck brought him in again drunk in his own piss and puke to sleep it off downstairs. I thought of how I'd feel if Richard ever reacted this way, and I was happy that he's never found out some of the things I've been doing.

Of course, the young worker and I hardly ever exchanged a word after that. We'd just used each other for an afternoon, that's all, and we both understood that. I wonder why most men can't be smart like him. But then what would I do to get what I want?

Love, Debra

October 13

Dear Mom,

I'm sorry I haven't written recently, but things are getting harder. Richard is getting worse.

He went to Welfare and of course got on, but since he told them he's an alcoholic he had to see their doctor. The doctor apparently saw something special about Richard and recommended that he try to get on Social Security Insurance for being disabled.

Richard thought this was ridiculous, but it was the only way he could stay on General Assistance. So he applied for SSI and they sent him for a psychiatric interview. Not knowing how to handle the interview, he just told the shrink the truth and even the shrink was impressed. He told Richard that he's both depressed and anxious, with perhaps a bit of schizophrenia to boot. He then told Richard that he was sure to qualify but in case he didn't, to definitely appeal.

Well, Mom, I've never seen Richard so happy, because GA is $301/month, but SSI is $620/month, which is more money than Richard has ever brought in.

All this would have been grand if the shrink's prognosis had been faulty, but Richard is getting more and more out there. He'll leap up from his book and start killing the phantoms before him in the most agonizing paroxysms. Sometimes I can yell at him and make him stop, but usually I can't get through. Then when the fantasy runs its course, Richard is in an altogether different room without knowing how he's arrived there. I'd like to say that this is the end of the fantasies, but once they start, they usually keep going at staggered intervals for some time. He tells me that he's killing people, ripping them apart and gouging out their eyes, horrible things. After one fantasy has run its course, Richard always says that's it, no more, but they always come back.

And as long as I've known him he's staggered and jumped around calling out "Flyball! Flyball!" as if he were an outfielder chasing one down. After many months of this he seemed to get some insight into "Flyball!" He told me that he had been a semi-pro baseball player and the last play he'd ever tried to make was to dive for a flyball, but the second baseman was running out for it as he was running in and when Richard dove for the ball, the second baseman kicked him in the head. Then it was nip and tuck whether or not Richard would survive. At first he was revived through artificial respiration, then he spent long weeks in the hospital followed by a lost summer because his memory was gone. He said that it came back to him slowly and he first became aware of himself just walking around his house in late August.

It interested him to discover now, in his Social Security psychological test, that he still can't memorize anything. Richard, who always reads everything he can find, tested as some kind of idiot.

Anyway, not long ago Richard came home with his back bent and in pain from a muscle spasm on Haight St. during one of his violent fantasies. He says if he keeps this up he'll have a heart attack. And he's afraid of acting out like this in the street for fear that someone might take him off as an easy mark, or the police will pick him up for the crazy bin.

And he's started wearing coveralls all the time. They're

too small and only go down to the top of his socks, and one side of his coveralls is held together by a piece of rope. And he's talking to himself a lot these days, like all the other red-bearded loons that wander around Haight St.

Mom, I have no idea what to do. I just have to accept what he's going through and pretend everybody isn't watching. Of course with all the nuts cracking around Haight St., it's pretty hard for anyone to stand out. There is always another clown drawing attention.

I try to talk to Richard when he's into his craziness, but nothing much gets communicated because Richard is in no position to listen to anything. I just have to tolerate this until Richard's demons quiet down.

I am a little bit afraid, Mom. Richard is not a violent man, at least not to me. He does things to hurt himself. I've seen him throw and break things, but he never hurts me. Still, I find him terribly unpredictable, so there's no way to be sure when he'll just use me as the victim of his fantasy.

I had a crushing blow recently, Mom, when I answered the phone and it was a woman. There was silence a long time before she asked for Richard. When Richard took the phone, I could see the agitation in his face. He carried the phone into the bathroom and shut the door so I couldn't hear him. And he was in there a long time.

Finally, after he'd hung up and returned to the living room, I asked him who he was talking to and he told me it was a friend of his from the Academy of Sciences, somebody I'd met once named Juno, a young pretty secretary in the geology department. I felt a rush of jealousy. I was even disturbed that she looked a lot like me, small and thin and moving like a tomboy. I asked him what she wanted. He thought awhile before saying that she wanted to talk about a relationship problem.

I tried to joke by saying, "You mean with you?"

But Richard winced like I'd hit him in the groin with an axe, and he turned very pale.

So I said, "Have you been seeing this woman?"

"What difference would that make to you?" Richard said softly. "You think I don't know how you've been fucking around since we've been out here?"

Well, maybe Richard knows more than I thought, but I doubt if he knows everything, so I dropped it.

Anyway, it was then that I knew how much I really love Richard and I went over to hug him to let him know this, but he wouldn't hug me back. He just stood there like a ragged totem pole, and Mom, I think I would have liked it better if he'd just knocked me down.

Love, Debra

November 7

Dear Mom,

I'm now almost always assigned upstairs at Oz, to help out in detox. The second floor is where the men and women go who are serious about drying out and getting themselves into programs.

At first I liked it because it's much more peaceful than the jungle downstairs, but it's still so hard to get to work in the mornings. I've been there several months now and it's hard seeing so many drunks come in and out. It seems that almost nobody makes it. Even the staff has a high rate of recidivism, because after you work with alkies awhile and you are one too, it seems that they suck you back into that old life again. It's really depressing.

Well, I start to work at 6:30 a.m., which is horrible enough, but one morning I got to the door and knocked to be let in and who did I see lying in the garage but my middle aged puppy sleeping it off, the one I left when I ran off to ball the young detox worker. I tried to wake him, to see if I could take him inside, but when he saw me he called me a slut and stumbled on away down the alley.

You see everything at Oz, Mom, but this devastated me. I

84

know better than to think I can make a man drink, but I felt I had played a major role in the life of this particular alkie whom I'd kissed in the laundry room.

I went to work and talked to Merritt, a counselor there. Of course I couldn't tell Merritt everything, but he told me to detach, that I can't make anybody sober and can't make anybody drink. Still I couldn't get what I'd done out of my mind, and just before I got off work that night we got the word that my middle aged true love had hemorrhaged and died in San Francisco General.

I thought of Richard and how I'd been mistreating him, and I knew what a horrible person I am, Mom. So I walked to this bar in the Tenderloin, and it was automatic. I had a john in 15 minutes. He was a visitor in from Seattle for some convention. So we went to the Hilton where he was staying and I came out of it with $75, but it didn't make me feel good.

I can't think of any time I've felt worse, not since coming to San Francisco anyway. I just started to walk up the hill on Mason and over past Chinatown down to Fisherman's Wharf. Then I went along the bay to the Marina and on past the Presidio all the way to Golden Gate Bridge.

I walked up onto the bridge and thought of all the people who have jumped. I looked down into the bay just as a big freighter was passing beneath me on out to sea. It would be easy, Mom, just to leave all this. It didn't look too far down. In a second you'd hit the water and it would be all over.

Then I got scared. I actually felt a force lifting my leg onto the rail. I was being driven to jump, Mom, and I didn't want to go like that. If not by natural causes, I at least wanted to check out by my own choice.

So I ran off the bridge and didn't stop running until I'd arrived at Lombard St. to catch the 43 bus home to the other side of the city. I let myself in our apartment and called for Richard but he wasn't there. Then I felt sick because I knew he was probably with his Junie.

I got into bed and pulled the covers over me. I could only

hope that Richard would come home that night. And I knew that was it with Oz, that I wouldn't be able to return. I'd tell Richard I was going to work, but instead I'd just go to the Wharf and turn tricks. I hated myself and what I felt I had to do, and I hated Richard too, because if he would just make a living maybe I wouldn't be forced into doing this.

I shut my eyes and tried to sleep, but I couldn't because I kept seeing you, Mom, and how you'd fix us breakfast sometimes when Daddy'd be passed out or at work. I loved you then more than at any other time, and I knew you'd never approve of what had become of me. And I'm sorry too, Mom, I really am, but I guess it's too late now.

Love, Debra

Dear Mom,

Richard did come home that night, and he was drunk. I just didn't know what to do. I went from loving him to hating him worse than I've ever hated anybody. He passed out on the floor before he could get to the bed.

I just got up and stepped over him. I got dressed and out the door to spend the night in the donut shop at 9th and Judah where all I did was cry.

I got back home exhausted after spending all night at the donut shop. I'd hoped to find Richard still passed out, but no, he was sitting up at the dining room table over a bottle of wine.

"You have to get rid of that damn thing," I told him, pointing at his quart bottle.

He said this was his house as much as mine and he'd have anything in it he damn well pleased. So I snatched the bottle off the table in front of him and went to the sink to pour it out. He screamed like a desperate cow and lunged across the kitchen to get his bottle.

I don't know how hard I hit him with it. It didn't seem that hard, but Richard went down like he'd been shot. I didn't really care. I just poured out his wine and called the MAP truck to come and get him and take him to Ozanam Detox.

It took MAP awhile to get here and Richard woke up too drunk to know I'd hit him. He asked if I knew about any wine he thought he had. I told him no and he sat back at the table to cry and ask me if I loved him. I told him that I did, which was true, but I hated him at the same time.

MAP arrived and I was surprised that Richard didn't complain. He just walked down whimpering how bad he was and let me and the MAP driver put him into the back of the truck for his trip to Oz.

Well, Mom, I just sat in the rocking chair and looked out the window most of the day, but I couldn't really see any-thing. I couldn't even think. Even though I was totally wasted I couldn't get myself to lie down on the mattress that Richard and I had shared all this time. I did open all the windows to let the stench of wine out and didn't care if I was cold. I was just glad Richard hadn't puked or pissed all over everything. And then I almost died, Mom, because there was Dad again sitting on the bed just staring at me. And he was all covered with blood and his flesh had wasted like wax to his bones, with all his teeth rotted out. I asked him what he wanted, but he didn't answer. And the more I looked at him the more he looked like Richard and I hated him. I could stand it just so long, Mom, before I took my teddybear and bolted out the door vowing to leave everything and never come back.

I walked through Golden Gate Park and must have looked a little weird because a cop on a horse stopped me in front of the De Young Museum to ask if I was all right. I told him I was and walked on, but I wasn't sure where I was going and my ears rang so loud I could barely hear the noises in the streets.

I didn't really become aware of where I was until I was standing beneath the bridge along the bay. I stared up for a long time thinking that sure was a long way to jump. Then I began to run again because I felt that old compulsion. But I stopped almost as soon as I began because I thought I saw something in the water bobbing close to the rocks along the shore. And I got terrified because it was a corpse, a girl who looked just like myself bobbing face down, and a seal swam past her not caring. Then, Mom, I began to see other corpses floating in the bay, all of them I'm sure suicides. And I looked up at the bridge and saw this man perched on the edge preparing to leap, and it was Richard. I yelled at him to get back but of course he couldn't hear me. Then he jumped, like a missile plummeting into the bay. I couldn't bear to watch him strike the water, so I started to run again. I knew what I wanted, some smack or coke or a goofball, anything to get away from myself.

And I found myself standing outside my body just gliding

along watching me race through the Presidio crying and gasping. And the more I observed myself the sillier it all became. None of this or anything else made any difference. Why did I care? Why did I care about myself or anything else? It was all this insane game, none of it to be taken seriously.

Then I woke up. I'd passed out in the woods of the Presidio behind a row of homes for Army personnel, and above me stood a little terrier yapping. I reached up and scratched him behind the ears as he wagged his tail.

I sat up and it took me awhile to recall all that had happened. Then I knew I had to get rational. The first thing I did was reach into my jeans to find I had no money. I knew I couldn't get myself to return to our apartment, even if I might find some money, which I probably wouldn't do anyway.

So knowing the first thing I had to do was to get money, I left the puppy and walked to this bar I knew to play some pool, and right away found this hooker with some coke. We shot it up in the bathroom and I came out feeling powerful and secure. Before the morning was out I had my john and $100 in my pocket.

Step two was down to the Greyhound station. I took the next bus I could find going north and found myself on my way to Fort Bragg. I thought that meant an Army base or something. I really didn't care. But I was really surprised when I ended up in this beautiful little town along the coast, with Georgia Pacific lumber company as its only business, along with a little tourism. It only has 5,000 people in it and I can walk from one side to the next in several minutes.

Of course that whole trip up the coast through the redwood country and up and around those big hills was more beautiful than anything I've ever seen before.

So I got out of the bus at Fort Bragg, and something said to me, Mom, that this was the place where I have to be. I only have about $75 left and the clothes I'm wearing, but that's enough.

I walked around the town awhile, all filled with these little frame houses, then went back to the main drag to sit in the Tradewinds Hotel restaurant for a hamburger and coffee. I looked at the pretty waitresses and wondered if I couldn't be one of them. I figured the motels probably had their hookers but it would be more a side activity here. Anyway, I just don't want to do it anymore. I didn't want to do it yesterday morning in San Francisco either, but I needed the money.

After my meal I took a walk to the other side of the highway that ran through the center of town and saw the old Skunk Railway with its ancient cars and locomotives. And I walked on through a viaduct to this field filled with all kinds of flowers along the shore. And I stood on the cliffs above the ocean beating on the rocks, and I've never seen the sea so blue, going from purple to green and aqua, washing over the tidepools and the sand.

I walked down the cliff along a sandy path until I was on the beach with the sandpipers and gulls, and I lay on the warm sand just looking up at the sky, and I knew everything was all right, Mom, that nothing could really hurt me anymore if I just remembered that I'm a part of all this.

Then I woke up and it was already dark with the moon and stars over me, and I sat up to find the tide almost risen to my feet, and I saw this thing that looked like a log rolling up and down with the surf just a few feet from me. I stood up to get closer to it and was shocked to see the carcass of a seal without a tail. Perhaps it was bitten off by a shark.

Suddenly it felt very cold and I walked back into town to end up sitting here in the lounge of the Tradewinds. For some reason nobody questions me being here. Maybe they feel sorry for this young girl.

By the time morning comes and I walk out of here, I'll be scared and lonely again and wonder what I'm doing in Fort Bragg where I know no one and have no income or place to stay.

Love, Debra

Dear Mom,

Just because I'm in a pretty little town doesn't mean that
things will necessarily change, not some things anyway.

I enjoyed walking around the town all day, but I really
didn't want to spend another night sleeping on the beach. As
beautiful as that was, I didn't want to find myself beside some
dead seal again. I talked to an old woman at the Tradewinds
and she assured me there are some rattlesnakes out there and
I'm just lucky to be alive. But neither did I want to use up
what's left of my money that has dwindled to below $50.

As I sat at my booth with a cup of coffee, wondering
where I would spend the night, this fat man in a blue suit
oozed into the seat across from me, where the old woman had
just been counseling me about rattlesnakes.

He was already looking at the menu when he asked me if
he could accompany me. I didn't say anything because I
didn't like him from the start. He was 50ish and pale and
nervous, and I kept feeling the grease might start rolling from
his hair down over his face. And even his heavy cologne was
not enough to cover his sweaty body odor.

He asked me if I wanted to eat, and I wasn't about to pass
up a freebee so I ordered a chicken dinner and a chocolate
malt. He told me that he'd seen me last night trying to stay
awake in the lobby and wondered if I had a place to stay. I
didn't trust him but I decided to feel him out for as much as I
could get off him. So I told him I was just in from San
Francisco with no money or job or place to stay but was
considering asking for a waitress job at the Tradewinds.

"Would you like to work for me?" he asked.

I didn't say anything.

He told me he was the manager of the hotel and he needed
maids just then. He asked me if I was good at making beds
and I told him I was. Well, he said, his name was Nick and I
could start work right away if I wanted. He'd pay minimum
wage plus give me a room.

I was in no position to say no, so after we ate and he'd paid for my dinner he took me out to show me my room. But it wasn't at the Tradewinds. He drove me to a smaller, run-down motel along Hwy. 1 where I discovered I had a room-mate, a young woman about my age. She was sleeping because it was already late, so I didn't meet her until we awoke the next morning. Her name is Ronnie and she's from a small town in Idaho, a pretty redhead but tired-looking all the time and a bit too skinny. I hope the job won't do that to me.

We worked together after having a small breakfast in a truck stop along the road. It was really pretty easy, but Ronnie seemed a little depressed and we didn't talk much.

Then it happened. Nick asked me to the office because he wanted to talk about something. As he smiled at me I could see that some of his tiny yellow teeth were missing in front, a real joy of a person.

"Debra," he said, "I want to give you a chance to make a little extra money here and get a little excitement at the same time."

I immediately hated him as much as he'd always disgusted me, because I already knew what he was going to ask. He wanted me to host some select visitors for the night, which would make me an extra $25 a night. "Who knows, Debra," he wheezed, "you might even find your next husband. We have a lot of important, wealthy men passing through this town."

I smiled. "You mean, they'd rather stop here than at the Tradewinds?"

He laughed slyly, "Well, you can see what we offer that the Tradewinds don't."

"I used to offer it back in San Francisco," I said, "but never for less than fifty."

He nodded. "I thought you might be a little experienced when I first saw you, Debra. That's good." He started nod-ding like a pigeon. "But you see, San Francisco is a more expensive town than Fort Bragg. What they do for fifty in San

92

Francisco, they do for twenty-five out here. You see, Debra, it's so much cheaper to live out here. You'll really be making more money here taking in twenty-five than you do in San Francisco for fifty."

"Forty is as low as I'll go."

"I'll protect you, honey, you know that. I screen everybody who comes in here looking for a girl."

"Forty."

We finally agreed on $35. It really isn't too bad with a free room thrown in. If I can't handle it I can just leave, Mom. Anyway, for now it seems like the right thing to do, since I'm almost broke and don't have another place to stay.

I went back to work and really crashed. I was back into it again, and I'd vowed never to touch a man again, much less this way. As we were cleaning up a room Ronnie smiled at me for the first time and said, "So I guess Nick just told you what this job is all about."

"Nothing surprises me," I said.

"It's not so bad," she said. "You ever hooked before?"

I told her that I had and she said it could be worse because Nick is a sonofabitch usually but at least he is good for his word. And it's never that active anyway, no more than two or three tricks a week, she says, even during the tourist season. It's actually a good way to save money, because there's no way to spend it at Fort Bragg, at least not too fast. She said she is saving it up so she can go back to Idaho and take care of her son who is 2 years old and living with her mother.

"I won't be here long," she said, "It's just that after Lonny left me, I had to do something. Really, it could be worse."

Well, I feel I can make it through a paycheck at least. After we get our work done, which sometimes doesn't take half the day, we're pretty free to wander around Fort Bragg or Mendocino or hike through the woods or along the ocean. Mom, I've done a lot worse.

Love, Debra

November 19

Dear Mom,

Ronnie introduced me to the best deal in Fort Bragg. It's called the Cookhouse, a restaurant not far from Nick's motel. $3.75 for breakfast and $7.50 for dinner, all you can eat. I think everybody along the Northern California coast must bring their families there to gorge out like pigs.

It's all cafeteria style and you can come back for seconds and thirds, just keep eating until they close down. I've gone there for dinner and had 3 chocolate sundaes and 4 pieces of chocolate cake, and nobody ever says anything.

But usually we go for breakfast. And we can choose from eggs to all kinds of sausage and bacon and french toast and pancakes and lots of fruit and cereal with all the coffee or juice I can drink, then come back for more. We both eat about six breakfasts apiece, then we fill our plates to the top one last time and when nobody's looking we pour the food into plastic bags we've picked up at Safeway, to be taken back to Nick's for dinner.

The trouble with this is I always know my food is there in my room, so I usually can't wait for dinner to eat it. That means I'm still hungry before the night is out, and I have to eat again at Tradewinds.

Ronnie is right about Nick. Even though he's disgusting he always pays you on time, and as long as you do your work he pretty much leaves you alone. Two other girls do what we do, both college students at College of the Redwoods, Janey and Sue, and they live together on the other side of the motel. They keep to themselves and are a pair, just like Ronnie and me.

But I've never had a friend like Ronnie, Mom. I guess she's the closest friend I've ever had, maybe the only real girlfriend I've had.

We got so close that we started sleeping together too, and the other day Ronnie said, "We're lesbians."

Well, I got kind of mad at this and said, "You can be a

94

lesbian if you want, but I'm a hooker."

And she said, "We can be lesbians and hookers at the same time."

So I said, "You can be a lesbian and hooker at the same time if you want, but I'm just a hooker."

"Then why do you sleep with me?" she asked.

And I said, "Because it's warmer and I like you."

"Well," she said, "that's what lesbians do."

And I said, "I don't care if that's what lesbians do. I do it too, but I'm still just a hooker."

So she said that was okay with her, and we curled up together and went to sleep.

Ronnie is right about the johns. We only get 2 or 3 party boys a week. One week I didn't get anybody and that was okay with me because I'm still saving up money, just like Ronnie said I would. After I got a stash of several hundred dollars I began to worry about it, so I opened a checking account at Bank of America. They asked for an ID and credit card and all I had was my fake ID but by then the town knew me, so they opened my account anyway and that's what small-town checking is all about. Just like the rest of small-town living, everybody knows everything about everybody and there can be a lot of love in that.

And Ronnie likes to walk a lot too, just like me, and she likes the forests and hills and the ocean. She isn't into a lot of things, like pretty clothes or a nice new car. Sometimes we talk about getting a car but we never do it. We do fine on foot or hitching to places like Mendocino or the state park beyond it. And at night sometimes we go to Caspar, a little town of a couple hundred people between Mendocino and Fort Bragg to hear music and dance at a bar. There are always a lot of nice guys there. They don't usually know that I'm a hooker and Ronnie's a lesbian. They take us home or we take them to our motel room sometimes and party all night. This is the one thing Nick doesn't seem to like, because they're always freebees and Nick gets nothing out of it. He also isn't sure they're freebees, like maybe we're ripping the poor fatman off.

Another thing Ronnie and I like to do is paint and draw. So we take our sketch pads and easels to the Mendocino coast like all the other artists there, and we draw and paint. Actually Ronnie likes to do this more than I do. What I do most is sit out there or in a coffeehouse or library and read. I read Pilgrim at Tinkers Creek and, Mom, I think Annie Dillard is the best writer in America, maybe the best there ever was, even better than Emily Bronte. Annie Dillard writes of the woods and things, like what we have here at Fort Bragg and Mendocino. And then I like to read Joan Didion and Jean Rhys because they write just like I feel so much of the time. And sometimes I feel just like a Jean Rhys trapped woman living alone with no money in a Paris hotel.

I think maybe I'd like to be a writer, Mom, but I'd like to do it more like Annie Dillard than Jean Rhys. In Dillard all life is as wonderful as it is beautiful and horrible. I read this little book by her about a little girl who has her face burnt off. One day she's fine and happy and the next she's in a hospital with her face destroyed. Well, I feel that's so much like me, like anything can happen to any one of us at any time, Mom, and we're just not in control, like the flies and moths caught in the spider web and devoured by the spiders in Annie Dillard's house.

But it's still as beautiful as it's mysterious, and the little girl still believes in God because God is everything and all around her. But God is also pretty horrible, Mom, and Annie Dillard understands this. She knows how horrible it is that you drank yourself to death and Daddy hurt me all the time. But she knows how beautiful and loving it was when we'd fix breakfast for each other when Daddy was away and we'd eat it together, just the two of us. And that's why Annie Dillard is the greatest writer, even greater than Emily Bronte, Mom.

Love, Debra

Dear Mom,

The inevitable happened. Ronnie was so proud of being a
lesbian and having a relationship with me, and I had to ruin it
by finding a man. I couldn't help it. It seems that after I left
Wisconsin I've always had one around. I loved Ronnie, I
really did, but she couldn't give me what I needed that I could
get only from a man.

Anyway, I met him one morning at Egghead Omelets
where I'd go when I wanted a place quieter than the Cookhouse. I was sitting over coffee reading this novel when the
man at the table next to mine asked if he could use my cream.

From there it got to him being new in town, because he'd
just been thrown out by his wife in Eureka because she'd
taken up with another man. I asked why he hadn't thrown her
out, and he said that he had 2 kids and felt it was better that
she keep the house with them in it. I asked why he couldn't
have kept the kids in the house with him in it, and if she had a
new man why couldn't she just move in with him. He said
that would be hard because the new man was living with his
own wife and 3 kids. It looked like we weren't going to
progress much in this discussion, so I asked him what he was
going to do in Fort Bragg.

He thought awhile and said, "I don't know. I just couldn't
get myself to stay in Eureka with my wife and her new man."

He said his name was Luke but he looked too gentle for a
Luke, like his mother had the wrong kid, but he was a good-
looking boy, maybe still in his 20's, small-boned and slight
with blond hair. And his slacks and plaid shirt were ironed
and his brown loafers were shined.

"What kind of work do you think I could get around
here?" he asked.

"Not the kind you're used to, I suppose. It's pretty depressed. Georgia Pacific isn't doing much. And that leaves
the service jobs in restaurants and motels mostly. It doesn't
pay too good."

He told me not to be deceived by the way he dressed, that he was used to bad-paying jobs because Eureka had been depressed for years and after losing his teaching job he'd been unemployed for most of a year. "That's the main reason my wife took up with that other man. She got tired of being the breadwinner."

I asked him what that other man did, and he told me he was a minister. "He's a good man really," he said, "but he fell in love with my wife."

"While having a wife and kids of his own," I said.

He laughed and said, "The flesh is weak, even for a minister."

So Luke and I spent all morning at the Egghead talking. I had to get back to Nick's to fix up a few rooms and this surprised Luke because he was staying at Nick's until he could find something a little more permanent that didn't cost much. He asked if he could take me to dinner later and I said yes.

Nick was a little mad because I was supposed to have fixed up the rooms earlier, but as it turned out there hadn't been that many rooms to do and Ronnie had done it all herself.

She asked me if I wanted to go to Mendocino with her and I said no because I had to stick around for my dinner date. I could tell she was a little disturbed but she didn't say anything. Instead she took off herself for Mendocino.

I read in my room until Luke knocked, and we went off to a nice restaurant in Mendocino overlooking the cove, and I listened to Luke roll out his life over bottle after bottle of wine. He grew up in Seattle and went to the University of Washington on a scholarship but dropped out before the end of his freshman year to ship out as a seaman for the next few years. Then he married his high school sweetheart who had graduated from college by then and was teaching. She got Luke to return to Washington to get a BA in elementary education. He taught then at the same school with his wife.

She taught kindergarten and he taught 3rd grade. But the stress got to him and he began to drink more and more until he started to miss work a lot and they fired him. He started to tell about his wife, when his head suddenly fell down to rest in his broiled trout.

It makes me wonder, Mom, just what is it about me that attracts all these drunks? Well, maybe everybody's a drunk, I don't know.

Love, Debra

December 6

Dear Mom,

Luke got lucky. He found himself a job right away as a janitor at Georgia Pacific. And he did something else that surprised me too. He bought an old school bus to live in and invited me to live there too, rent free.

He went right to work taking the seats out of his bus, leaving only the back row to sit in. And he bought a mattress at the Salvation Army as our first piece of furniture. And he found a couple of empty plastic jugs behind the Safeway to wash out and fill up with water to drink on the bus, and he bought some toilet paper to use after going to the toilet in the woods. And every time he decided we needed something more, like cans of tunafish, he bought it as cheap as possible, like a sheet and a couple heavy blankets and a sleeping bag at a garage sale.

We were sleeping in there one night in our place off the road in the woods, when we heard this noise outside. A couple of men tried to get in the bus until Luke yelled about getting the gun we don't have and the men ran away.

Anyway, first thing next morning, Luke got a heavy padlock at the hardware store and rigged up a way to put the lock on our door, either outside or on the inside when we would be sleeping. It turns out, Mom, that Luke is pretty handy with mechanical things and he loves making a home out of our school bus.

But he said it bothers him having to go to the bathroom in the woods and then burying the toilet paper. A lot of people wouldn't bother to bury the paper, Mom, but Luke is into preserving the environment, which means we can leave our crap where it lies but we always have to bury our paper.

Anyway, Luke found an old toilet lying beside Hwy. 1, so he picked it up and put it in the bus and we drove it back to our spot in the woods. Then he dug this deep hole and put our new porcelain toilet in it. It's pretty low to the ground but at least it's better than the way we've been handling it, and Luke figures we can let nature flush it when it rains. He always feels the best way to do anything is to let nature be the guide.

Love, Debra

December 27

Dear Mom,

Those were some of the best few weeks of my life, Mom. I spent as little time at the motel as possible, because I was always with Luke helping him fix up the bus. But now it's ended like everything else in my life. Luke started to drink. He came back to the bus with a case of liquor, then warned me that once he got started I'd better get lost for awhile.

I've had enough experience to know what that's all about but still I hung in there. After the first few swallows from the bottle, Luke was happy and giggling and we danced around the bus celebrating our new home. But then after a few more swallows he just sat on the steps of the bus and looked thoughtful. Then he got somber and grumbled a lot. Then he started to talk to his wife, like she was right there arguing with him about something. I just sat back in a chair I'd put

100

under a tree, and the more I watched this plunge into insanity the sadder I got.

Then he was looking out of one eye, because I knew he couldn't focus out of both at the same time, and he looked at me and called me his wife. It's when he leaped up and accused me of fornicating with the minister that I knew I'd better get out of there.

So when he went for his shovel to lop off my head I leaped up and ran down the road. I looked back to see him coming after me with the shovel, but I saw him stumble and fall, he was so drunk. I just kept going the 3 or 4 miles back to the motel to find that Nick had a party boy for me. I was glad of this because it was my revenge on Luke.

Somebody told me later that Luke came to town to scream up and down Franklin St. until the police collected him for a night in jail. And then they found out that he was wanted in Eureka for more than just skipping out on his wife. And that's the last I ever saw or want to see of Luke.

Ronnie was pretty mad at me for awhile and I didn't much blame her. We worked together cleaning up the rooms but she wouldn't talk to me. I asked her to go paint with me off the cliffs in Mendocino and she said no. I also asked her to the movies, and she said I could take myself to the movies. And I can't tell you how many times I apologized. I'd try to sneak into bed with her, and she'd shove me out to go sleep in the other bed.

At last I was really desperate and I offered her my teddybear, the one Richard had given me back in Chicago, my one and only faithful friend for years. That's when Ronnie stopped pouting and really started to cry, because she knew how much that teddybear meant to me. So I got in bed with her and held her and later we hitched to Mendocino to paint and I bought her pizza at the deli. And I kept my teddybear too.

Love, Debra

January 3

Dear Mom,

When Ronnie learned that I was getting $35 a trick from Nick, she was really mad, because she'd been working this motel a good deal longer than I had and was only getting $30. We both agreed this was outrageous and stepped over to this bar on Hwy. 1 to pick us up a couple johns to take back to our motel room for $50 a head. Of course, we did them extra favors like switching partners and playing some exotic sex games to keep them interested, but we didn't get any of this through Nick so we weren't going to give him any of our earnings.

The next morning when Ronnie and I were making up the beds, both of us more than a little hung over, Nick came by to ask us about the party we had last night.

At first, neither Ronnie nor I said anything because this wasn't any of Nick's business at all, but I could tell from looking at him that we might get hurt unless we made up something. So I told him they were a couple friends of mine and weren't for money.

Then Nick was really mad because he said he knew the men we partied. They had been there a couple weeks ago with the two college girls working the other side of the motel and Nick wanted to see the money he knew we took in last night.

Well, people like Nick can be pretty scary when they're mad. And I could tell that Ronnie was pretty scared, but I had no will to share any of my $50 with Nick. So when Nick turned toward Ronnie I swung a pail of water at him and bounced him full on the side of the head. Down the fatman went like he'd been killed, and Ronnie and I were out of there fast.

We didn't bother to go to our rooms, there was no time. We ran to Franklin St. and another couple of blocks to the apartment of a dike truck driver friend of Ronnie's. Fortunately she was there and let us in. Ronnie told big Lou what we had just done, and Lou asked if the police might get in on

102

this. I told her I didn't think so because Nick wouldn't want to blow the cover on his cathouse, even though the Fort Bragg police had to know what was going on anyway, but I'm sure part of the arrangement was the place had to be quiet and never make trouble. So Nick would rather lose a couple hookers than get busted.

So Lou, who might not have known anything herself but had to pretend like she did, said I was right and the thing to do was ride with her that night to Eureka because she had a pick-up there. Then Ronnie and I could stay with a friend of Lou's until we could think of something better to do.

We didn't have much choice but to go along. So that night when Fort Bragg slept, Lou drove her big truck to her apartment and Ronnie and I slipped into the back as her cargo and in a few hours we were in Eureka.

Lou took us to her friend Skinny Ernie who owns a slum bar in Old Town, and Skinny Ernie put us both to work in his joint as bartenders and since he owns the whole building he gave us a room in the hotel above the bar. It's even wilder and more rundown than the Farling in Chicago but we don't mind. Ronnie opens the bar in the morning and I work with Skinny Ernie on the afternoon shift.

It isn't that hard really, just serving a few old derelicts who cash their social security or retirement checks and drink their money away before passing out on the bar. The average age in the joint, I believe, must be around 60.

The trouble with Eureka is that it's flat, depressed and ugly. There's no place to go but Old Town, which isn't as big or nice as Old Town in Chicago. It's a combination of skid row and an arty section, which means a couple bookstores, an amateur theater, an old fixed-up hotel and a few fancy restaurants and shops all mixed in with a gang of winos and skidrow bars and flops. What this means is that we stay drunk and drugged all the time to pretend we aren't even in Eureka.

Our life seldom extends beyond our bar and hotel. We work and drink all day, then pass out in our room at night.

It makes me think of you, Mom. I really don't want to live my life and die this way.

Love, Debra

Dear Mom,
Eureka is the biggest trap I've ever been in. I wake up in the morning with Ronnie and we can't talk because we both need a drink so bad from drinking all the previous day and night. So I go down with her to unlock the bar and the first thing we do is pour us both big glasses of vodka. And of course the old wineheads are waiting at the door and some of them are in worse shape than we are.

Ronnie doesn't even ask them what they want because she already knows. That's how they know how much she loves them, because she knows what to pour for their morning wakeup—Donny a shot of Four Feathers with beer wash, old Dirk a glass of muscatel, PeeWee a vodka in a tall glass with a straw because he's shaking too much to pick it up to his lips.

Almost nobody says anything. And nobody has to pay for the first one either, that's understood. Also the tv goes on. The tv has to be going all the time, day and night, even if nobody's watching it. It starts with the Good Morning show and progresses to the daytime soaps and game shows, then on to the afternoon movie. It doesn't make any difference what's on because nobody is in any shape to watch it, but still it can't go off.

After my glass of vodka and a few minutes with my head bobbing in the San Francisco Chronicle to see what the President's doing to get us into war in Central America while giving the country away to the filthy rich and attempting to drill for oil everywhere off every American coast, I either have a beer and hardboiled egg with maybe a slimjim for

104

breakfast, or I get my daily exercise by walking 3 blocks to a depressed little diner for their special of 2 eggs over easy and hashbrowns.

There are many days when this is my only meal of the day, except for slimjims, hardtack and hardboiled eggs at the bar. On Sundays I'm forced to vary the routine because my diner is closed and I have to walk 5 blocks to an even more depressed restaurant—but there the special is 2 eggs and 2 pancakes and the coffee is thrown in too, all for $1.99.

I look at the movie section of the paper a lot, and when the local paper gets delivered Ronnie and I decide on what movie we might go to that night, but we never go because Ronnie will be too drunk after sipping vodka all afternoon on my shift and I'm too tired after an afternoon of labor. So all I want to do is sit on the stool beside her for a couple vodkas and beers to relax.

We seldom remember much of an evening and we discuss not knowing anything that went on after my shift ended, because it's all blackout drinking. We never know how we get upstairs and into our room, and we don't know a thing until the desk clerk gives us our horrible wakeup call at 5:30 a.m. because Ronnie has to open the bar at 6:00.

We never have a day off but neither do we ask for one, because as horrible and dull as it is there's nothing else we care to do but sit in that bar and guzzle Skinny Ernie's booze for nothing. Skinny Ernie doesn't mind because that's all he ever does too.

Now comes the catastrophe. Ronnie just got a letter that her mother is sick in Idaho and Ronnie has to go home and take care of her kid until her mother gets well. This terrifies Ronnie because even though she talks about wanting to see her kid she hasn't done this in such a long time that she doesn't even know what the child looks like.

"What if he doesn't like me?" Ronnie whines. "What if he doesn't know I'm his mother? I think he's three now, maybe four, oh god, oh god."

Well, Mom, this whining went on all the time we got

Ronnie packed and ready to go. I was relieved when Ernie and I finally got her on a plane at Eureka to transfer at Eugene, then Portland and on to Boise where Ronnie would be met by an uncle with her kid.

But then my own loneliness began because Ronnie was my only friend in Eureka and the only other person I knew was Skinny Ernie who immediately put the make on me—because his wife of 20 years hated him and I was the only person in the world who understood.

The next morning I awoke with Skinny Ernie and it was no different from waking with Ronnie, but I guessed it was better than waking with nobody because that thought was too scary. The trouble was that Ernie breathed in my face, and the combination of his cigars with the morning after made him repulsive. What we did the night before doesn't make any difference because I'll never recall any of it anyway.

Skinny Ernie is a bent beanpole with a faceless kind of loose skin and terror. It's hard to look away from his eyes that pop from around a long thin nose with terrible desperation. He never talks in full sentences. He says, "The beer!" which means fill the beer cooler, or "Vodka!" which usually means give him a glass of vodka fast before he collapses. And if I don't understand his one word of command and stand too long trying to figure it out, he gets mad and grumbles, "Slut!" or "Pigwhore!" which is both his favorite and longest word—until he gets just far enough in the bag that he starts to bad-mouth his wife and tell me how much he needs me. This too rolls out with no sentences, just a steady stream of garbled abuse for her and roses for me.

Well, Mom, without Ronnie there I got more and more desperate. I buried all this in booze—until one morning I awoke in a strange place. It wasn't my room in the hotel with Skinny Ernie breathing on me. I was lying on the floor of a cell with four other derelict women screaming all around me.

They took us before the judge and I can't recall too much, but the judge directed most of his rage toward me because it seems that I had flipped out and drunkenly demolished

Skinny Ernie's bar with a baseball bat. Skinny Ernie was at court to scream at me until the judge had him thrown out. As for me, I was sentenced not to jail but to deportation. They gave me a Greyhound ticket for anywhere in the state, paid for by the City of Eureka, as long as I never came back to that sad city.

In an hour, with 2 Safeway shopping bags filled with everything that remained of my life, I was on a Greyhound back to San Francisco.

Love, Debra

                                          January 28
Dear Mom,
When I got off at the San Francisco Greyhound depot I was exhausted. I hadn't really gotten much sleep at the Eureka jail. Anyway, the only thing I could think of to do was to call Richard and hope he was sober. He answered the phone and obviously was, and right away he invited me home without me even asking. He was overjoyed that I had returned and things would be different now. I asked him if he was sober and he told me he'd been clean and sober now a couple months and was taking AA seriously this time.

So I walked over to Market St. and caught the N Judah subway train and was at Richard's in half an hour. I still had the key, so I let myself in and there was Richard standing in the hallway smiling at me.

I put my shopping bags down, horrified. "My god, Richard," I said, "you look wasted!"

He stepped forward to embrace me and replied, "That's a helluva way to greet your old daddy after all this time."

I wouldn't let him hug me. I pushed him away and said, "You're sure you've been sober?"

"Look," he said throwing his hands up, "I'm sure I've been sober two months, like I said." But then he looked suspicious. "Hey, *you* look like you've been thrashed and baled. What's been happening with you?"

I told him about Fort Bragg and Eureka and how I'd just been deported back here.

"Uh huh," he nodded. "You ask me about my sobriety, *you're* the one with the problem, my sweet child."

"It's always been different with me, Richard," I defended myself. "I've always been in control. I've always been able to take it or leave it alone, depending on how good or bad my life's going."

"Sure," Richard said, going to the rocking chair to sit down. "Since your life has always been bad, how do you know how you'd be with life going good?"

"Well," I said, "I had a few good weeks in Fort Bragg, and I didn't have to drink or use then."

"Sure," he said, "sure!"

The longer I looked at him the worse he seemed to get. I'd never seen his eyes sunken into such swollen bags, and he'd obviously lost a lot of weight. "Good god, Richard," I moaned, "you used to have some meat on your bones. What happened to it?"

He laughed. "I haven't been able to eat much."

"Why not?" I asked. "What happened?"

"Well," he said, trying to act jolly, "after you disappeared and I got sober again—which I did on my own, incidentally, just me and AA, no hospitalizations—I caught what I thought was a bad case of withdrawal, but it held on too long and I thought it was some form of the flu, which it may have been, but it wouldn't go away. And then I noticed some spots on my body and got worried. So I went to San Francisco General for some tests." He stopped talking.

I waited awhile before asking, "Okay, you've had some tests, and what did they find out?"

He answered quietly and deliberately. "I have AIDS."

It was hard registering. "AIDS! You?"

"Yes."

"Well, Richard, why you? You don't pick up faggots on Castro St. I've never seen you use a needle!"

He smiled and said, "So why should I bother you with everything I've ever done? Have I asked you to account for every minute of your time? I know how you've lived your life, Debra. I haven't wanted to know the details of everything."

I shook my head. "You've balled a faggot?"

"I don't ball gays!" He paused like he really didn't want to tell me. "But there have been times when you have been doing your thing when I've sought the company of a decent woman. And, yes, maybe I shared a needle."

I felt the jealousy raging. "You mean that floozy secretary at the Academy?"

"I don't think Juno would have given me anything. I've told her about the others. She doesn't test positive. And I could have been exposed years ago."

"Well, what about me?" I howled. "Have you exposed me to anything?"

He started to get angry. "The way you live, it could have been a million guys! Go to General and check yourself out if you're worried!"

Suddenly I sat down on the mattress and stared at him. "Oh my god!"

"My god what?"

"Poor Richard." I went to him and put my arms around his skinny frame. "I'm sorry."

"Well, you won't have to be sorry long." He started to cry. "I'm sorry, Deb. It's just that you're the first person I've been able to cry to about all this."

I held him for several minutes as he sat in the rocking chair, before I stood back and said, "Well, how long will it be then?"

Richard looked down sadly. "They don't know. I guess they never know for sure. I guess some can stay alive pretty long." He laughed softly. "I don't know if that's good though, not the way I feel sometimes. Of course, I'm still too scared not to keep going as long as possible."

I held him again and we cried together for a long time.

Love, Debra

Dear Mom,

I think my greatest shock about Richard is to see this man, once a robust 180 lbs., now wasted to about 125, and he's very weak and tired most of the time. The apartment was filthy. Richard has always cleaned it before because I never wanted to, but I cleaned it this time, even washing all the floors, cleaning the toilet, everything.

While I was doing this, Richard sat in the rocking chair and tried to read, but he couldn't manage more than 5 minutes without falling asleep.

And there was almost nothing in the refrigerator, certainly not enough to make a meal, not even an egg. And all around were empty pizza and Chinese food cartons, so Richard had been sending out a lot.

So I went to McCambridge Market a few blocks away and did my first real shopping. Richard had always done it when I'd been living here before.

Fortunately Richard had hooked into his SSI, because I had no money. Still it was only $620 a month and I knew I'd have to bring in some money if I expected to live there and help Richard.

I bought hamburger because I know I'm a master at making hamburgers, and I bought cheese and onions too, to make them real good for Richard. And I bought catsup and buns, everything. I wasn't wise enough to purchase more than one meal, so tomorrow I'll find nothing for breakfast but at least I did well for tonight.

I fixed Richard a big hamburger rare, because I knew

that's how he likes it, and gave it to him in his rocking chair. He laughed and thanked me but he couldn't eat it. He just held it a long time and occasionally broke off a tiny piece from the bun to put in his mouth.

So I asked him how well he'd been eating and he told me he hadn't felt like it.

"Richard," I said, "eating is necessary for us all. It's how we fuel our little bodies. It's how we make the bones and muscles grow."

He didn't laugh. He grumbled, "Thanks, Mommy."

I took the hamburger from him and said, "Would you handle it better if I fed it to you?"

"You mean like a little kid?"

"Yes, like a baby."

"Well," he chortled, "to tell the truth, I might just like that."

So I shoved the hamburger up to his mouth and he took a bite. It took him a long time to chew it up and swallow, but then he said goo goo and I shoved another bite into his mouth. It took him forever to get it chewed and swallowed, then he held his hand up to block his mouth against bite three.

"Would you like some ice cream?" I asked.

"Not particularly."

"I bought strawberry, the kind you always liked."

"You bought it for me?"

"You know I like chocolate fudge, of course I bought it for you."

"Then I'd better have some."

So Richard ate a small bowl of ice cream that I fed him while talking baby talk. It was all a game, we both knew that, but Richard had always liked to play games, so I got him to eat his ice cream.

Finally I said, "Richard, how were you able to manage when I was away?"

He giggled. "Not too well the past week or so, but that's because I'm a little weaker." Then he got serious. "But I would have managed somehow without you. I always have."

111

"I know," I admitted. "I guess I was for the most part a burden on you."

He reached out and stroked my hand with skinny fingers. "Without the burden of you around, my life would have been totally meaningless."

"What do you mean?" I asked.

"I mean, I love you, Debra."

"You're kidding!"

"Why do you think I ate the hamburger and the ice cream?"

We laughed and I held his hand as he slept.

Love, Debra

March 15

Dear Mom,

Taking care of Richard takes its toll on me. I go from feeling like Superwoman Nurse Jane to being mad and resentful that I can't do anything but take care of an invalid, and sometimes Richard gets self-pitying and threatens to commit suicide. I always talk him out of it but it's all a game and I know it. I should tell Richard to do it and if he needs help I'll always be there for him. Then I feel guilty for letting thoughts like this in.

Also, Richard's SSI money always gets used up before half the month is out and I have to get some more in the best way I know how, which means going to that bar on Fisherman's Wharf and taking on my old role. I resent Richard for that too, but it's still the easiest quickest way I know of to bring in a few dollars. And I didn't have to work long at it. A couple of days of 3 or 4 johns and I make more than Richard's monthly SSI provides.

I don't tell Richard where I'm going when I get dressed for work, but of course he knows. It's the only time I ever put on the high heeled/short skirt/heavy makeup costume and the only time I ever carry my red bag. (Of course, I never put anything valuable in that bag, certainly no money, because I never know what fingers will find their way in there.)

Still I recall the first time I was about to go to work, after Richard's money had been spent and Richard whimpered from the rocking chair, "I don't want you to do that."

Aggravated I turned on him. "Do what?" I asked.

"Go back out there," he said. "You and I both know what."

"Richard," I said, "it's so nice of you to be protective of me, but we're broke. Maybe you don't like to eat, but it's one of my favorite habits."

He got angry. "Don't get funny with me about your favorite habits! I have an income, we can make do on it!"

I tried to be patient. "I'm glad you have an income, Richard, but it's not enough for one to live on, much less two. Now don't worry, it only takes me a couple hours when I get started, and we can have steak tonight."

"You'll be too fucked up. You'll take your pills, smoke a few joints and drink up the bar!"

"I only do enough to get through. You know I can't do it straight. Look, Richard, some things just have to be done, and I don't want to talk about it anymore, okay?"

"I saw the way you looked when you came back from Eureka. I don't want you that way."

"Who said I wanted *you* in any way, Richard?" I walked out and shut the door, but when I got to the head of the stairs I wanted to go back and apologize. It made no sense to be cruel to him. It was all hard enough anyway. But I couldn't get myself to return and resume a conversation on the horrible thing I was doing.

I had a pretty good day, three tricks before 2:00 p.m. and over $200 in my pocket. I would have gone home, but Richard was right. I was too fucked up and it was all I could do to walk out of the bar.

Somehow I woke up sleeping in the grass of Aquatic Park, and the miracle is that no one had ripped me off. I still had

113

my bag and the wad of bills buttoned into a pocket of my skirt. I walked to a ladies room in Ghirardelli Sq. and cried when I looked at my face in the mirror. It was horrible with makeup smeared all over, and I was bloated. I'd put on weight.

So rather than go home I wandered up Polk St. feeling a little hung over and crashy. I went to a thrift shop on Sutter where I bought jeans and sneakers and a men's plaid work-shirt. I walked out of the thrift shop looking like a dike, anything not to think of what I'd just done.

I bought steaks and a few other things at McCambridge and took them home to Richard, who decided not to talk to me. He was watching tv which he almost never did before, but reading is getting difficult for him. It's hard for him to focus his eyes and he's too weak to hold a book up for any length of time.

Well, I'm getting pretty good at simple cooking, so I prepared us some steaks, rare like Richard likes them, and I mashed some potatoes and made a salad. Then I cut up Richard's steak into bites small enough for him to handle and started to feed him as he watched tv. Even though chewing and swallowing is getting to be a task, he ate a couple bites of steak and rudely spit the third bite onto the floor.

"Godammit, Richard!" I wailed, "I've done all this for you, and you treat me like a pig!"

"That's because you *are* a pig," he grumbled.

I put his plate down on the floor and covered my face with my hands to weep, until I felt Richard's hand on my arm and looked at him with a river of tears coursing down his left cheek.

"I'm sorry, Debra," he trembled. "You're not the pig, I'm the pig."

So I hugged him pressing my face into his bony breast. "Richard, forgive me, it's just so hard to do all this when you're sick. It wasn't long ago that we were in Chicago and you were taking care of *me*."

"I know, Debra, we take care of each other." He let his

face down to rest on my hair.

Suddenly I had an idea. I straightened up and smiled at him. "I've got it, Richard, I know what we should do. Let's go to the beach like we used to do."

At first he looked happy, then sad. "I don't know if I'm strong enough."

"Look, Richard, you'll only know if you try. I'll help you walk the three blocks to catch the N Judah to the beach, and then when we get off it's just a few feet to the viaduct that goes to the beach, and we can sit there like we used to do and just watch the waves break up at us. I'll even collect shells for you if you want."

He laughed. "I think I'd prefer you just sitting beside me with my arm around you, and we can cuddle."

"Okay, Richard, let's cuddle."

So off we went. It took forever for Richard to get down our stairs and out the door, but when we reached the sidewalk, he cheered up because it was a victory. Then with his left arm over my shoulders and his right hand carrying a cane, we worked our way to the stop in front of the donut shop. The train arrived a little before we did, but the trainman was nice enough to wait for us, and two people got out of the front seat so Richard and I could sit down right away.

Richard didn't talk all the way to the beach but he was looking out the window and laughing. It's the first time I've seen him happy since I returned from Eureka.

Richard was shaking by the time we made it under the viaduct onto the beach, but even as weak and exhausted as he was he insisted that we walk through the sand to the edge of the surf where we both kind of collapsed like ragdolls laughing.

We sat holding each other for a long time just looking out at the magnificent sea, as the sanderlings raced before us pecking through the surf for a meal and the sky kept turning colors.

I felt his tears on my face and looked at him. "Are you okay?"

115

"Oh, I'm okay," he said. "I'm more okay right now than I've ever been sitting out here with you. But it's all so sad."

"I know, Richard, I know."

"I don't mean my sickness, I mean everything. That's what the sea is telling us. That's what it's always trying to tell us, it's all so sad."

I tried to think. "Yes, Richard, I guess it is."

And then, Mom, I wanted to die. I thought I wouldn't make it as long as Richard, I really didn't!

Love, Debra

March 30

Dear Mom,

Richard is getting worse fast. Some people hold on for a long time with AIDS, I've been told, 4 or 5 years, maybe even a little longer. Others have gone as fast as 2 weeks. Of course it's really hard to tell, because it might be a late diagnosis. But still it isn't too hard to tell that Richard is going fast.

The best I can do is to get clinical, like a nurse. I can't afford to think of Richard as my best friend because then I'll perish ahead of him.

That trip to the beach was our last. It was our last outing anywhere. After sitting out there for 2 hours, we could never have gotten home if we hadn't found a kind man walking his dog to watch the sunset. Because he helped me carry Richard to his car and drove us back to our apartment and then he helped me carry Richard up to our apartment where I got Richard into bed.

The very next day I had to make arrangements to get a wheelchair because it was the only way to get Richard around in the apartment. And he was slurring his speech and having a hard time putting a thought together. At times he would forget my name or think I was somebody else. I stopped correcting him. If he called me Sue I was Sue. If he called me Mother I was Mother. That's what I'd become, Richard's mother. I didn't resent the role because I was paying him back for playing father for me so long.

The hardest time is when I have to leave, because he gets scared and thinks I'm abandoning him, and when he knows I'm going out to turn a trick he clears up enough to be enraged and tell me never to come home again. This really hurts because the only reason I'm doing it is to support Richard. I hate it but Richard is getting even more expensive the sicker he gets. As a matter of fact, Mom, my whole life is for Richard. He is my only reason for living anymore.

At times breathing gets hard for him and I am sure he is dying, but he always settles down somehow and his breathing returns to normal. As the days go by he sleeps more and more and he watches the hated tv because that's all he can do. Except he likes me to read to him. He requested King Lear because he's decided he is King Lear. I can't read more than a couple pages before he's asleep. So it's slow going.

At night I carefully wash away the men I've been with. I scrub myself clean because I hate them so much, and even though Richard is beyond interest in sex I'm purifying myself for him. And I crawl into bed beside him and press against him, resting my arm over the skeleton that was once so well-muscled. And that's how I think of him too, as my muscular daddy in Chicago.

Several times I've thought he was gone and I turn on the light to find him still breathing, still with me. Once he woke when I was looking down on him, and he knew what I was thinking because he winked and said, "I'm okay, love, go to sleep."

At first I cried a lot but I usually tried to keep it from Richard. I wanted to be honest about my feelings with him but I didn't want him to know how much all this tortured me. I didn't want him to feel more of a burden than he already was. But the tears dried up with the feelings and I went on

117

automatic, doing and feeling all the right things at the right times. Still I don't know how much longer I can hold up this way. I'm exhausted and irritable and I take it out on my johns. One started to beat me I made him so angry. Fortunately somebody knocked on our hotel room door and that quieted him. But I got out of there as fast as I could, not even waiting to be paid. I vow to find him someday though, Mom, to get back somehow.

Still, with Richard I always want to be gentle and giving. Richard said in one of his clearer moments, "Why don't you just let me die?"

"I don't know," I said honestly. "Is that what you want?"

"You know, Debra, it's okay, this dying, I've been at it long enough to know. Sometimes in my sleep my brother comes to visit me."

"I didn't know you had a brother."

He smiled. "You don't know because we hardly ever talk about me."

Then I felt sad because it's true. Until recently I've never taken enough interest to get to know Richard. We've always been working on *my* problems.

"My brother died years ago in Korea," Richard said. "Then I think my mother died of grief. I was the family bum, and my brother Samuel, he was the hero. He'd gone all the way through the University of Illinois to become an accountant, and I'd dropped out of high school to join the army. But it was my brother, not me, that was killed in Korea. My mother, of course, blamed me for this."

Richard was beginning to fade off into sleep, so I shook him a little, because I had to hear about his brother.

"Well," Richard said tiredly, "he just said it was all right, and I could let go now."

"Which means?"

"You know what it means, Debra. It means I can let go, and it's all right."

Richard was asleep, and I stared at him a long time, because I knew he was leaving me soon and I was glad it was all right for him. But I don't know if it will be all right for me. I turned off the light and pressed in against him, and I think I cried the rest of the night while he slept.

Love, Debra

April 22

Dear Mom,

Richard stopped eating and started pissing in the bed. I didn't know what to do until I phoned San Francisco General and they told me about this hospice for AIDS patients run by the Catholic Church. I was lucky that they had a bed available, and Richard became the only straight man in there.

I would sit by his bed and talk to him, but I don't think he understood too much by then. I bought him flowers, because he used to buy me flowers, and I let him have the teddybear that he bought for me in Chicago, the one thing I always had with me. Richard may not have known Teddybear was with him giving him hugs, but he was. And I never stopped holding his hand because I felt maybe that kept him aware of my presence.

His breathing became uneven and strained and sometimes it would stop altogether. Then I'd say to him, "It's okay, Richard, you can let go now." But for some reason he couldn't, because the breathing would begin again and sometimes I felt pressure on my hand like he knew he was holding mine.

When it became apparent that he couldn't possibly get through another night, I was allowed to stay with him and they brought me something to eat along with Richard's meal. Richard hadn't eaten more than a bite, it seems, in days. And I found that I couldn't eat either.

I'd brought him a balloon because I recalled way back at the Farling Hotel how Richard and I would bat a balloon back and forth in the office in the middle of the night when the rest of the hotel was sleeping. I tied our silver balloon to his wrist and let it fly over him and for some reason I said, "See your silver balloon, Richard? That's your spirit. It's okay, you can let go and it will fly up to Heaven, because that's where it wants to be now."

And I know you'll find this hard to believe, Mom, but I saw Richard rise from his body and he winked and whispered, "I love you, Debra." And off he went, just like a balloon.

I held his hand awhile longer but I could already tell that it wasn't Richard—the face, the body, none of it was Richard. And I could see the wasted bones beneath the blanket and was grateful that Richard was now freed of them.

So I untied the balloon from Richard's wrist and gave him a kiss on the forehead, then carried the balloon and Teddybear outside. I had no idea what time it was but it was sunny and beautiful, and I walked over into the playground beside the church to see a group of gay men playing softball. Then I walked a few steps into the outfield and looked up to say, "Here's your balloon, Richard. You can play with it now." And I let it go to watch it go up up into the blue sky, and as it danced around with the wind I knew that Richard was with it, hitting it up and down, embracing it, and I waved to him and he waved back. I watched the balloon until it was a speck and then disappeared altogether, and then I knew Richard was all right, he was on his way.

So I walked to the corner of Diamond and 18th off toward Castro. But when I got to the South China Cafe a gay man stepped out right in front of me. We stared at each other for awhile, and I'd never seen the man before but he embraced me and we cried together for a long time, almost like he knew what I'd been going through. When we finally released each other, I thanked him and walked off and never saw him again.

I stopped at Castro St. and suddenly felt so alone. Richard was gone. I had no place to go. Even if I went back to the apartment I'd have to leave it. It was Richard's apartment but now they'd rent it to somebody else. I couldn't bear the thought of going back there anyway, much less living there.

I had Teddybear, and that's everything I'd want out of the apartment anyway. I was just glad Teddybear was able to be with Richard in his last days.

So Teddybear and I started to walk. My mind went mercifully dead and the only thing I could do was squeeze Teddybear and make my feet move.

And there I was again, standing beneath the bridge, looking over San Francisco Bay. How many thousands had jumped from that bridge and how few had survived. Maybe this was the time. I could put Teddybear down and some child would be sure to find him. He'd get a much better home that way, better than being raised by a hooker anyway. It would be easy enough. Nobody would much care. I'd get an inch in the Chronicle as an unidentified young girl who jumped off the bridge. I'd already read that article several times. It would describe me briefly and ask for someone to identify me. Of course there would be no one to identify me because no one cared.

It's then that I looked up, and way above me flew the silver balloon, a lot like a bird being thrown to the wind, and I really started to cry this time because I knew it was Richard and Richard cared. And I picked up Teddybear because I knew I couldn't just leave him after all, because if Richard cared about me I had to care about Teddybear.

Well, Mom, I looked through my pockets to discover that I was broke as usual, and I thought of going to the Wharf to find a john but I looked back up at Richard's balloon still hovering over me and I could hear him telling me not to do it, that I didn't have to do that anymore. And I waved at him and said, "Thank you, Richard, I won't." And I don't know why I did this, Mom, but standing not too far from me was this man in a blue suit, looking like a business executive and just staring out over the bay. I guessed he was about Richard's age.

Anyway I went to him and said, "Excuse me, my name is Debra. I know you can't possibly believe this, but…" and as fast as I could talk I told him everything about me and Richard. And then I said, "So you see, I'm broke, but I think I have a friend in Fort Bragg. If I can get to Fort Bragg, I'll be okay." I was lying, Mom, but I just had to get out of San Francisco. I couldn't stand it one more day.

But the man smiled and said he had a daughter in North Carolina he didn't see very much, because she was living with his first wife, and he gave me two $20 bills, then changed his mind and gave me another $10 as well. I thanked him and started to walk away but he called me back.

"Here," he said, giving me his card, "call me either at home or at my business address if you need anything. If Fort Bragg doesn't work out, maybe we can think of something where I live in San Rafael. I don't know, of course. I'd have to consult with my wife and two cats, but you never know. Life is pretty strange."

I agreed that life was pretty strange, then shook his hand and thanked him again and walked off along the Bay. I looked up one last time to see Richard, but the balloon was gone, so I guess Richard felt I was in good hands now. And, Mom, I hope you are too.

Love, Debra

Books of Poetry
by
Fritz Hamilton

The Street and the Joint

The Plunge

Redman is Redman's Mommy

Sores and Roses

A Father at a Soldier's Grave

No Difference

Beneath the Rags

About the Author

Fritz Hamilton was born in Chicago, Illinois, in 1936. He has a BA in Philosophy and an MA in English/Education from Roosevelt University.

After spending some early years as a teacher and social worker, Mr. Hamilton has devoted his full attention to writing.

While having lived many years in both New York and Chicago, Mr. Hamilton now resides in San Francisco with painter and poet Phoebe Grigg.

He has previously published seven books of poetry and over 1,000 poems, stories, articles and reviews in literary magazines and anthologies.